NAME THAT MOON!

NAME THAT MOON!

ROBERT ONOPA

DEUXMERS

Published by Deuxmers, LLC
PO Box 437305, Kamuela, HI 96743
deuxmers.com

"The Grateful Dead," "The Lights," "Name that Moon," "The Swan," "Traffic," "Republic," "The Atchison, Topeka & Santa Fe" and "Geropods" originally appeared in *The Magazine of Fantasy & Science Fiction*; "Blue Flyers" originally appeared in *Tomorrow.*

Printed in the United States of America.
ISBN: 978-1-944521-23-3 (Softcover)
ISBN: 978-1-944521-39-4 (Ebook)
First edition, October 21, 2024

CONTENTS

INTRODUCTION: WHY SCIENCE FICTION?

Why science fiction? Why read it? Why write it? Let me describe two reasons to do so, motives at the heart of science fiction's appeal.

First, there's the way the genre exposes both reader and writer to the absolute wonder of the cosmos as it's revealed, layer by layer like a sweet Maui onion, by contemporary science. Bear with me as I describe a piece I read this morning. According to an article in *Nature*, it is tantalizingly difficult to pin down, on the most precise level of detail, where life begins. At the level of atoms, for instance, there isn't any proof of life at all, since atoms are just assemblages of electrically charged particles whirling in space. (As a footnote, remind yourself that an atom therefore consists mainly of the room between the particles, so the average atom is more than 99.99 percent void.)

Atoms are the constituents of molecules, which gets us closer to life, but even if molecules are "organic," that doesn't make them actually alive.

We have to take another step up, to where billions of molecules come together to form parts of single cells, parts that produce proteins, parts that are able to reproduce themselves, before we get something we're willing to call life.

Now that's still not my life or yours, not by a long shot (though sometimes we might feel a bit single-celled first thing in the morning). It takes around thirty trillion cells, each made up of trillions of atoms, to construct one of our living, breathing, human bodies.

Did you keep the proportion of empty space in atoms in mind? Think about what that means, about how delicately insubstantial our material reality is. Think about the magnitude of those numbers. They make you catch your breath, or wave your arms like the late Carl Sagan, as you might in the presence of the sublime. Equally wondrous is the way billions of those cells in our bodies are swapped out every day, recomprised of atoms and molecules from the air we breathe, the tea we drink, the dinner we eat. We physically re-make ourselves all the time—our skeletons, for example, are never more than ten years old. We have a structure that remembers which atom goes where, which is how we renew ourselves, how life goes on.

At least as extraordinary is that most of the basic building blocks of our bodies, the electrons and protons and neutrons of the atoms, are some twelve billion years old, nearly as old as the universe itself. Simple atoms came early in the evolution of the universe, more complex ones slightly later, forged in stars and supernovas, ejected into space, then coalesced by gravity into our solar system, our home planet, and, eventually, you and me. All the constituents of that hand of yours or your eyes or those of your loved ones are more than ten billion years old, and the classic science fiction writers had it right when they told us that it is of star stuff we are made.

The sense of marvel that these observations inspire is part of the appeal of science fiction. This kind of material is difficult, almost impossible, to integrate into any other art form—dance, painting, poetry, sculpture, architecture or realistic fiction—though this material is, when it comes down to it, the real world itself.

Science fiction invites us to join with Immanuel Kant, who said that two things alone gave him constant cause for wonder: the starry firmament above and the moral law within. In the way science fiction tells human stories against a background of scientific inquiry, advance, and speculation, it is the only art form in which the reader and writer are invited to participate in both.

So then, along with illuminating the starry firmament, the second reason for science fiction's appeal is its unique power to integrate contemporary science with fundamental human stories, stories whose rhythms pulse with the heartbeat of life as we experience it emotionally and ethically.

Here's an example. A few years ago I was watching the full moon rise from the Pacific at Kalama Beach, near where I live in Hawaii. I was listening to friends, executives in the hotel business, complain about a slump in tourism. The sight of that bright celestial sphere, the meandering conversation, generated the title story of this collection for me, a story set in the near future at a failing resort on the moon, a gentle satire on tourism and the human side of travel in a difficult economy. Once I started the story, I found myself searching out moon maps, downloading data and images from the NASA sites on the web, and when I'd made some basic geographical decisions, spending hours on my lanai gazing at our grand natural satellite. I needed, after all, to observe and contemplate the site near the Menelaus Crater I'd selected for my story's resort, and I had to track the route my escaping lovers would take through the Plinius highlands down to the Sea of Tranquility and the Apollo 11 site. This kind of research, perfect from a rattan lounge chair on clear Hawaiian nights, kept me in the story, I'm sure, longer than I needed to be. But there was another, interesting result.

When I looked into what it would be like to walk on and drive over the moon's surface, it turned out that the closest parallel on Earth, the very place the Apollo 11 astronauts had used to train for their own journeys, was in my own backyard. The Apollo 11 voyagers had trained in Haleakala Crater, a high caldera, a Manhattan-sized expanse of cinder cones, lava flows and dusty, regolith-like lowlands, that crowns the eastern half of the island of Maui. Haleakala happens to be one of my favorite places to hike and camp—I've been going up there for fifty years, and I'd just been up there a few months earlier with my wife and boys. The story led me back to our days in the caldera, recalling the crunch of cinders beneath my feet, the thin air in my lungs, the sublime sight of high cliffs and giant cinder cones, the pleasure of being with my family on one of our adventures. In the course of working on the piece, science fiction had put me in the cosmos in a spiritual way, had literally raised my vision, while intimately connecting it to my own human story.

There's more, of course, that science fiction can do. It can shape character, promote social change, encourage technical innovation, extrapolate a future, poke fun at our failings, and alter the way we see ourselves. It can stimulate, frighten, reform, and even make us laugh. But somewhere in the course of the story it tells, genuine science fiction casts a proprietary magic, a power to inspire wonder, to connect us to the very origins of the universe and the creation of the stars, even as it leads us from the heavens back down to Earth with a renewed sense of the richness of our own lives.

(A previous version of this essay appeared in the New Zealand magazine *Salient*.)

THE SWAN

The column of black smoke was visible from ten clicks away, dense and billowy, shifting in the wind like a dye marker in ocean currents.

Photochemical colors in the twilight sky: mauve and filthy pink. The old Army turbocopter rattled through the airspace above coastal LA, descending gradually toward the source of the smoke in Long Beach Harbor. Standing in the open door of the copter's cargo area, one hand on a safety strap, Voorst squinted south through the haze at the continuous string of makeshift harbors where houseboats seemed every year to multiply like algae in a pond. He guessed densities of five or six thousand per square kilometer, half the rigs illegals, population out of hand.

The way the picture was never seen on CBS or VNN ate away at him like an ulcer. As they swung upwind of the column of smoke—it hung below them now three thousand feet like some fantastic butte in Monument Valley—he pulled himself across the cabin, took a deep breath, then leaned out the opposite cargo door, trying to make out what was going on near the source. The pattern of debris and smudge spread clearly from a large ship, one he maybe recognized: rusty white decks, an out-of-service pool, a blue hull—a passenger liner auctioned off years ago and anchored in the harbor as one of the transient hotels, the QE 3.

The copter weaved down alongside the column and his stomach tightened, the sensation like floating down a precipice untethered. Now he could make out the big Virtual News Net uplink out on the breakwater. The shoreside traffic was gridlocked, the sea lanes so crowded even a SoCal Harbor Inspector like himself (but what did Harbor Inspectors matter anymore?) had to hitch a ride through the air.

This was the third harbor fire in a week. One up in LA proper, the other down in Balboa.

A soft wall of black came rushing up and they wafted into the smoke. In the darkness the copter's interior screens brightened and he checked the image going out over VNN—he was used to the way they altered a landscape, accustomed to seeing some of the live-aboard scows bled out of harbor shots, but now it looked like they'd moved the source of the fire too. On the VNN screen the smoke rose from a Brazilian bulk carrier anchored in the industrial harbor northwest. Voorst ground his teeth. The acrid edge to the air belonged to burning petrochemicals, not the cargo of Amazon mahogany whose loss the smooth-voiced anchorman was describing. Still, even the VNN summary screen showed the crowd—people with bundles, transients being driven off—fighting with Army cops. "Hey, Stringer," Voorst shouted against the whine of the turborotor "*Stringer*. Your men gonna have the area secured by nightfall?"

The fiftyish sergeant, his name in block letters above the left pocket of his fatigues, seemed not to hear, didn't even open his eyes. He leaned against the bulkhead, the bank of internal screens glowing yellow behind him, and continued the story he'd started before Voorst had leaned out the door. "So I tell the lunchmeat I'm a friendly, right? I get her inside the troop carrier. There's nobody around. I get her on the floor in the back..."

Voorst grunted and peered out as the copter punched beyond the dense smoke, the light like a change of season. Elevation two thousand feet. The dusty sun lay above the horizon less than an hour from setting. "If you don't get secured," he yelled to Stringer, "you're gonna have another three, four hundred dead by morning. Look down there, you can see them swarming—people in the water..."

"C'mon," Stringer said. "Just listen: so when I take her

blouse off. She's holding must be three hundred housing vouchers? I clap the restraints on her wrists, got 'em threaded around the weapons rack. Next thing I know like her brain fuses, she goes twitch wild. I think, well, the zimmer likes the restraints, right?" The copter lurched in a wave of heat; a red light flashed at the back of the cargo hold, matched by a flush infusing Stringer's square, hairless face. "I go to pull off my holster and belt?"

Only now does the Harbor Inspector, Voorst, look carefully at the mangled mass of cartilage at the side of Stringer's head. "Something tells me I don't want to hear how you lost it."

"I didn't *lose* my ear. She *bit* it off. I mean, what are these people turning into?" Stringer pulled himself up and peered out the open door, holding the safety rails so tightly his knuckles showed white. "Man, what *was* this place?"

"South of the industrial harbor, see? A big old passenger ship—Harbors database shows upper decks were a Sears-Daiei Mall and a transit center, maybe two thousand people below. VNN's saying Nomads came aboard a bulk carrier, set a fire, the people in the harbor started looting… Jesus, they treat people like cattle."

"Nobody treats *me* like cattle," Stringer grinned. "What's the matter, pal? You afraid my people gonna hit you with the prods?"

Voorst looked at him: red-eyed, one-eared. He took a deep breath: petrochemical air. "Stay out of my way, Stringer," Voorst said, trying to keep calm. "I've got a job to do down there and I don't want your men interfering. Stay out of my way."

Voorst's job was to clear the harbor of illegal vessels. The first step was to identify the most dangerously unseaworthy craft, hulls he'd mark with his orange "V" for the Corps of Engineers to impound and sink along the massive net of breakwaters. Most of the few vessels which could actually sail had done so when the fire had broken out, just sailed north out of the harbor mouth to some other mooring. The illegals left behind ranged from slimy inflatables rigged as sleeping quarters, to makeshift houseboats with small kitchens, to old tanker hulls that had been converted into twelve-story "apartments."

Walking the docks, by sunset he found only six boats he could clear.

Two hours later he heard an appeal from a group of unwashed men and women and let slide the regs for a dozen trimarans moored under the tattered flag of the Ponape Yacht Club. Even as they spoke an illegal barge ghosted into an area he'd already inspected—the harbor changing amoeba-like around him. Still, he'd see to it the worst cases were sunk.

At midnight Voorst found himself picking his way across the deck of a converted cattle ship docked near the VNN uplink. Behind him the Corps was already towing the first hull he'd marked. Now he stopped to watch the Army drive a crowd along the shore back through the lurid light. The water was littered with clothing, cooking utensils, bedding. The red plastic of a toy Mars Rover crackled beneath his feet when he shifted his weight.

His heart went out to the people who needed a place to live, but what else could he do? When the big winter storms came slamming in from the Pacific, as they would in a month, the great breakwater itself a mile out wouldn't hold back the rising seas. Even in good weather the utility hookups were rats' nests and sewage fouled the waters for a click out. When the storms came, the collisions, capsizings, swampings—sheer overcrowding in the harbors killed thousands every year on this part of the California coast alone.

Voorst sighed, looked around to take his bearings. He'd covered all of the northern quarter of the harbor except for a crumbling pier near shore. He told himself that's where he'd quit for the night.

He walked over. He started writing off a string of listing hundred-foot hulks, sheet metal and wallboard shacks on scow hulls, when he realized that one rusty hull, partly sunk, was blocking a dozen small boats moored to a pontoon dock along a hidden channel.

That's where he found the Swan.

◇

She was an antique sailboat, a racing sloop from the 20th Century, Scandinavian-built, about forty feet on the waterline. He'd seen a boat like her in the museum in San Francisco once: a glass hull with fine, fast lines, a flush teak deck for quick sail changes, a tall mast with a narrow crosstree. Her gull-winged cockpit set her apart from other old racing boats and gave her away even from beneath a thick layer of grime. He'd never forgotten the words etched on the steel plaque in San Francisco: NAUTOR SWAN.

This boat's reg numbers didn't show up on his readout. She certainly was run-down: filthy, her decks gouged, her brightwork the washed-out color of driftwood. Her winches were crusted over and her rigging hung from the mast like an old spider's web. But there was no disguising the heart-breaking sleekness of her design.

"*Hello*!" Voorst called out from dockside, banging on the hull, hearing the fatigue in his voice. "*Ahoy the Swan*."

The boat had lost its rudder, seemed a bit low in the water. Still, he couldn't just have her sunk. He calculated his alternatives and started writing out a warning notice to post on the hull when he heard the companionway hatch scrape open on its tracks. The hair rose on the back of his neck—in the red glow from a secondary fire, the harbor had turned weirdly quiet; he hadn't met anyone for an hour.

And now a girl emerged from the low cabin. She was wearing a T-shirt of a provocative blue beneath a khaki wind-breaker. She was slim-hipped, high-cheeked, and pretty, but certainly just a girl. He guessed from the look on her face that she would have disappeared had she anywhere to go.

"Are you Army?" she said. Her skin was smooth as a mannequin's. Her hair was honey-colored despite the Oriental fold in her eyes and the flatness of her nose—someone's exotic, beautiful daughter.

"SoCal Harbors Office. Where's your family?"

"I'm older than I look," she told him, lips tight. "Try twenty-two. Are you going to squander all the boats in the harbor? The way you did up in Seattle?"

He grunted. "Who told you that?"

"Everyone knows about it. There's a pinch, the boats get condemned. The next thing you see, they're sunk at anchor. Then the bay gets filled in by some developer and apartment blocks go up."

The story bothered him too. The trouble in Seattle, as he recalled, had been a petrochemical slick that had unfortunately ignited at the turning of the tide. "We're not sinking anybody at anchor," he told her. "You're mistaking me for the FedHarbors people. But for your own safety..."

His device squawked and he stopped, took a message from ComNet: FEMA had scheduled a briefing at the fire's source on Dock G North at 0600.

He'd had to look down to read the message display and to shut his pager off. When he looked back up, the girl was gone.

◇

At the morning briefing—he'd been right about the source, it was the Queen Elizabeth 3, a floating flophouse belowdecks, the mall above—the Long Beach fire chief showed Voorst and the Army Evac Team where the blaze had started in the video department of the Daiei store, around 4 p.m. on the previous day. Someone had set off a case of Lydex, the Army's "sticky napalm," fragments of the original container blown out into a passageway. The Lydex—left over from the "police action" in Mexico—was the signature of the New Nomad Terrs, Stringer chimed in during his five minutes: Stringer was apparently something of an expert on the terrorists, Voorst was surprised to learn. Stringer's assistant placed the disruption to the QE 3's ComNet channel at 1602 hours.

"So they lost video uplink from this ship from the *start*?" Voorst asked.

A Black firewoman from Long Beach shook her head. "No way."

Stringer looked annoyed. "That's what the scum do first, blow the links, give you false signals," he said, but the Black woman only shrugged.

Voorst waited until the briefing was concluded and Stringer and his team drifted away.

"Show me," Voorst said to the firewoman in the yellow slicker.

Up forward in the old first class theater one of the Virtual News Network's "experience" rooms was still more or less in working condition, running three walls out of four. Voorst played back the holotape of what had gone out over the Net even before they'd flown out from Malibu, cutting the volume on the anchorman Tachikara's familiar, avuncular voice. There it was again: the QE 3 fire was already superimposed on the Brazilian bulk cargo carrier, the SEA ANGEL, anchored in the industrial harbor just northwest. He'd seen that harbor choked with live-aboards too as they'd flown over, but as he watched the walls around him projecting VNN's three-dimensional coverage, half the residential boats were gone, erased, digitalized out. Even the odor of the fire they were sending out over the Virtual Net was different, yes, incense sweet, a hint of burning wood from the tropics.

He supposed they had their reasons. Maybe the police had a lead on the Nomad Terrorists which would be blown if everyone knew the truth. Still…

"You believe this shit, what they do nowadays?" Voorst asked the Black woman.

She seemed rapt—on the screen, against the dramatic sights and sounds of the fire, a guy wearing a red bandana was pulling a comatose, semi-nude blonde out of water so oily it threatened to ignite. "This is better than what happened, man. I like this better."

Behind the slosh of the water and the crackle of flaming

lumber and paint blistering a hatch, an announcer murmured the station ID for VNN: *Here's There*! he said. *You're Here*! Voorst picked up the unerased string of scow hulls as part of the background on a side screen. Without giving it much thought he called up the screen controls and instructed the virtual-reality program to zoom in.

You could hardly see the edit lines. Blue shirts swarming near a derelict sailboat. The Swan.

"Hey," the Black woman said, "lookit that. Maybe those're the guys who started the fire."

Voorst shrugged. "Look at their bedrolls. Folded in a hurry. Look how those two are half-dressed, their survival packs a mess. That bunch is clearing out like they don't know what's going on."

The Corps of Engineers had already brought in two large cranes, and now a dredge from the nearby Naval Shipyard was stationed in the harbor mouth. The harbor looked trashed – debris strewn, littered with derelict vessels, scum on the water thicker than usual – but because the Army'd come in strength, the transients weren't swarming back as they had in Balboa, so today his own job seemed less urgent. Voorst ate a late breakfast with the Long Beach fire crew, a druggy bunch who shared Stim tabs with their coffee. Then he worked the Alamitos end of the bay out of a Zodiac for a while. Before long his eyes were burning from some toxicity in the air. He moored the Zodiac at an empty slip and walked over to the Swan.

The Eurasian girl was kneeling on deck, scrubbing corrosion from a winch with a wire brush. The boat was still grimy, black-streaked along the waterline from the frayed truck tires used as fenders, but metal fittings shone along the route of the starboard running rigging.

"It's a start," Voorst said.

She grinned nervously. On the mast she'd posted the Provisional Seaworthiness Certificate he'd left on deck the night before. "I'm obliged for the thirty days," she said.

Voorst nodded toward the scow hull blocking the channel. "That hulk should be towed out tomorrow."

Now her smile relaxed. "F'ntastic," she said. "That's the one problem I could never solve. I've got propulsion—a set of metal film sails that've never seen wind, a cranky methanol inboard..."

He couldn't quite place her accent: was she a refugee from the fall of Hong Kong? He was impressed, as she went on, by what she knew about sailing, by her ambition to take the boat out single-handed. "What are you going to do for a rudder?" he asked.

She told him the original rudder was at the bottom of the harbor, just below the stern. "It's a long story. My old boyfriend..."

"... left when the fire started on the QE 3," Voorst told her. "You can see that on the VNN tape."

Now it was her turn to be surprised. "I'm the one who found this boat to begin with," she said. "Stuck this way, filled with a dead man's kip. All Dana did was lose the rudder when he tried to make room for a stabilizing vane he never did attach."

"So what are you going to do about the rudder?"

"Dive for it," she answered, grimacing at the slimy water.

Voorst nodded. "You're going to need some help."

She flushed, started to say no, I don't, but something in her peripheral vision caught her attention. Voorst tracked her line of sight to a moving group a hundred meters away, above the debris-strewn beach, near a barricaded ramp to the docks: an Army patrol was prodding along fifty or sixty people dressed in the dingy old clothes of the homeless. The sergeant sauntering behind them hefted on his shoulder the distinctive barbed shape of a burn gun, the cruelest of the weapons.

Now the infrared gun was waved, in a familiar way, at Voorst. He spit into the dark water.

"I'm sorry I thought you were one of them," the Eurasian girl said.

Voorst ran his hand over a piece of coaming, thinking it

just needed to be scraped, sanded, and coated to look like new. During the night he'd dreamed of the Swan far out at sea, beyond the greasy slicks and floating carcasses, heeled over in a stiff, open-ocean breeze. "Well, if you need some help. I'd like to see this boat saved, see? I'd like to see you sail out of here."

"Look," she said, still watching the patrol on shore, "those soldiers make me nervous. You might as well come aboard."

Voorst stepped over a sagging lifeline and followed her down the companionway, not expecting much. But he found antique wood paneling, blue curtains shading the ports, a spotless galley. The beamy cabin was a museum of old-time comforts like teak book racks and built-in lockers. From the oversize electronics at the aft Nav station he guessed that the boat had last been seriously cruised fifty years before, around the turn of the 21st century. "My name's Rawley Voorst," he told her.

"So I gathered from the notice. I'm Tiana Parker."

He saw the T-shirt she'd been wearing the previous night on the forepeak bunk. "Isn't it kind of dangerous to wear Nomad blue?"

She shook her head. "They're just people without places to live, for Christ's sake."

"Or people who set fires with Lydex."

"If you believe that..."

"It's not a religion," he said, "It's not a matter of belief." He realized he was repeating sentences he'd heard on the Net, and caught his breath. "You must watch CBS or VNN. You must listen to journalists like Tachikara..."

"I suppose you believe everything you see on VNN?"

"No ... This is what I mean: they can manipulate the screens, but an anchorman like Tachikara with a reputation to protect, he's not going to fabricate..."

"Unless he's a construct, unless he's fabricated himself by the Crays at VNN every day. Tako Tachikara. Christ."

He'd heard rumors. "VNN," he sighed.

"The technology's a miracle," she admitted, pulling off

her workshirt, uncovering a sleeveless top and skin that glowed gold in the warm cabin light. "You know what would be splendid? Get some of that equipment, put it to use for human things. You know, people's memories… Make a holotape of teaching a child how to walk, or fixing this boat up." She leaned back against a bulkhead. "But they never let ordinary people get their hands on the equipment."

"They know how dangerous it would be to turn an unedited camera on the cardboard shacks of East LA…" In the silence after he spoke, he could feel the hull bob gently from some disturbance in the harbor.

"I'd be very grateful if you did help me," she said.

He thought he heard someone knocking around outside. "What do you need?" he asked her.

"For starters, do you know how to mend an electronic compass?"

Footsteps sounded above on deck. Voorst pulled himself up the companionway to find that the weapon-waving sergeant who'd been hiking on the shore, and who'd made his way, alone, across the littered beach, through a barricade, and across a series of jammed-together decks to land on the Swan's, was someone he knew.

"Hi," Stringer said, looking past him to the girl, smiling unctuously. "Hi, zimmer."

"Jesus," Voorst said. "You're gonna get your other ear bitten off."

"Gimme a break," Stringer said. "I've been up all night. My own men are startin' to smell as bad as the people we move." He smiled at Tiana, looking down into the cabin. "Nice in there."

She only nodded, fear in her eyes.

"We're here to protect you, see. I'm Sergeant Stringer. Where you goin' when Rawley throws you off your boat?"

"I wasn't aware he was," she said.

Stringer nodded sympathetically. "Well," he said, "you are now." He rubbed the stubble on his chin. "We're like brothers, see…"

"Like Cain and Abel," Voorst laughed.

Now Stringer bit his lip. "Who the fuck're they?"

Voorst shook his head. "Abel was a shepherd—say, Sergeant, does that make him the first Nomad? Anyway—you'll like this part—his brother Cain murdered him."

"Well hey," Stringer said, "people do get pissed off, right? Anyway, lunchmeat, get your pack. Ol' Sergeant Stringer's gonna take you in for a while."

"Don't listen to him," Voorst told her. "He's got two sexual assault convictions. One more and he's gelded. That's not a chance he's going to take."

"Zimmer still needs a place to sleep."

"Can't you read the provisional certificate on the mast?" Voorst asked with flat menace. "She's got as much right to stay here as you do in the West Hollywood Barracks. Or should we have a talk with your parole officer?"

Stringer flushed. "You can't pull that shit on me. This whole coast's goin' to be wasted before thirty days. Not even a duck's goin' to float here. Believe me."

"What are you talking about?"

"I'm sayin' you don't know shit," Stringer told Voorst with a sweaty grin, swinging back up the companionway.

◇

Like a graceful creature emerging from a chrysalis, Voorst thought when he returned the next day to see that the afterdeck had been scrubbed and oiled well enough for the grain of its teak planking to emerge. Up forward, a stay of bright new wire supported the mast and the bowsprit was freshly painted bright red.

"I couldn't sleep properly," Tiana admitted. "I kept thinking he'd show up again."

Voorst told her he knew his man, it wouldn't happen.

"What's in the crates?"

With the scow hull towed away, he'd been able to motor the Zodiac into the channel. He'd cannibalized, off one of the half-sunk tugs, a speech-synthesized Nav system. He stepped down and passed it up to her with a set of alloy turning blocks and a coil of fresh synthetic line. He saved what he considered his real triumph for last, a shoulder-mounted, double-lensed apparatus in a padded aluminum case.

"That's registered VNN gear," she murmured. "Where in the world..."

"I had a little help from a friend. Someone in the Long Beach Fire Department. It's a portable unit got left behind at the QE 3 site."

He'd set aside the afternoon to help her work. Even playing with the holocam, with just a few additional repairs a seaworthy boat started taking shape. They spliced new line onto the frayed end of a jib halyard and fed it through the masthead pulley to set up the running rigging. Voorst free-dived with weights into the murky water and found the rudder—which Tiana pulled up and he reattached with new alloy pins. Amid a floating patch of food waste and filth he scoured the harbor's muck from the hull with ultrasonic gear. By the time she had the tiller box packed with lube and turning freely, he de-filmed and scrubbed his own skin. If the Nomads who'd been on the boat were anywhere nearby, he saw no sign of them, or of Stringer. The harbor was strangely quiet, the air still throughout the hot afternoon.

When Voorst set the boom in the old gooseneck, sweat dripping from his eyebrows, he looked up to find she'd focused the holocorder on him.

"The boat, Tiana, the boat."

She set the camera down with a smile. "Dinnertime," she said.

In the west the sun was indeed low in a sky feverishly bright with unnatural pastels.

In the cabin below a sturdy fold-out table occupied the center of the U-shaped settee adjacent to the galley. She served him warm cabbage soup, brown bread, and soycakes, what he was sure Stringer would call Nomad food, just the diet of the poor.

At dusk, Voorst ran a line for the topping lift through the masthead and attached the bitter end to the boom. "Look this over," he told Tiana. "You're ready to hoist your sails." As she tested the rig he faced the harbor. The sky in the west had taken on an ugly, bruised quality, and in the gathering darkness fifty or sixty dim lights marked where families had reboarded illegal ships; he could hear muted voices and the dull metallic sounds of secret dinners being prepared. "I guess electronics are next," he said. "I'll be back in the morning."

She put a tanned hand on his forearm. "Please stay. Stay the night."

She had intelligent eyes, coal-black, and she was wearing a woman's scent. When he thought about the trip up to Malibu and his sleeping cubicle at the barracks, his bones just felt heavy. What was in Malibu? Three or four hours of VNN risk games stuck in a room with fifty soldiers plugged in like electronic components and breathing bad air.

Tiana didn't seem like just a girl anymore. While he took his second shower of the day she initiated sex like a woman of experience. Afterwards in the forepeak bunk she fell asleep, her arm across his naked chest. Only then did she appear vulnerable, as delicate as the small bones on the inside of her wrist. Who are you? He whispered in the quiet of the night. Voorst could sense the distant rhythm of the open ocean through the Swan's hull, the rising and falling of the swells. The sleep into which he fell was dreamless, deeper than he'd had in years.

On Friday morning, the explosions started at eight sharp, just as Voorst was punching up the code for dispatch to schedule his day's work for SoCal Harbors.

The concussions shook the air, sloshed water up the dock pontoons, sent debris and smoke a hundred feet high across the southern end of the harbor. Voorst braced himself against the ComNet dish he'd only just bolted onto the stern.

Another set of concussions—like a giant walking heavily along the far edge of the harbor.

Tiana looked up from the stanchion she was cleaning, gripping it tightly with one hand, breathing deeply.

"Not an accident," he said. "Look at the color of the smoke. It's white. I don't think it's an accident." When dispatch came up on his device, he told them to put him through to the FEMA office. He was using the ComNet dish he'd just installed as an uplink, noticed idly that it worked fine.

Sweat stung his eyes as he listened.

"There are people on those boats," he told the FEMA administrator. "I saw them last night." The argument was brief, punctuated by another pair of concussions.

"What *is* it?" she begged when he started throwing his gear together. On shore a crowd of homeless had gathered to watch the smoke. They were passive, listless—even though the Army was surely on its way with prods.

"The Corps of Engineers condemned the south end of the harbor," he told her.

Her eyes widened with recognition. "The explosions. They're sinking the boats at anchor. They drive the people out, sink their boats, fill in the harbor for apartment blocks… It's like Seattle."

"Not quite," he insisted. "There's no petrofire here. The main channel is clear. There's no cause for what they're doing. I'm going up to Sacramento and stop those bastards."

"Don't leave me."

"It's my job," he said. "Look: the Corps' finished for the day. At the rate they're working, you're safe at this end of the harbor for weeks. I'll be back tomorrow. It's my job, Tiana—everybody else is lying about this—FEMA, the Army, FedHarbors, VNN, the Corps of Engineers. I've got to try and stop them."

◇

Up in Sacramento he had to endure hour-long waits on worn-out chairs in Interior Department reception rooms whose false-landscape windows shimmered painfully with waterfalls and snowy mountains. Accumulated errors in their virtual-reality programs—entire sections dropped out of forests and cliffs, pixels burned sickening shades of blue-green—made his eyes water. The bureaucrats in their gray offices, speaking their foggy language, made his temples ache. But by the end of the day, meeting with the California Harbormaster himself in his office in the capitol, Voorst felt vindicated. The balding man's window wall might continue to display its retouched version of San Francisco Bay, but he agreed: *The harbor at Long Beach was SoCal's largest facility, an irreplaceable resource. The Corps of Engineers data was faulty.*

With the help of Lieutenant Governor Yasubu, at seven in the evening the Army Corp of Engineers was ordered, through Fed Interior, to cease demolition forthwith, pending disclosure that the harbor was unnavigable due to wreckage, blocked channels, or fully documented siltation.

Voorst dined with the balding man, an old tanker captain, in the executive cafeteria. Afterwards it was too late for a lift back to Malibu, so he accepted a barracks cubicle for the night. Stretching out on the narrow cot, Voorst felt exultant. The fantasy he'd entertained on his way up to Sacramento that morning, the fantasy of turning back and sailing the Swan to the South Pacific with Tiana, now seemed petty and selfish. The South Pacific had its own problems anyhow, a vast archipelago irradiated by the Chinese, a toxic zone below Johnston Island where a nerve gas disposal facility had failed.

Even when the Swan was fully refitted, he might not miss sailing away with her after all, wherever she was headed, he thought.

Until he found a holostick tucked into the bottom of his duffel.

He searched out an empty VNN experience room at the base Officer's Mess. The stick she'd slipped among his work clothes was the footage they'd shot working on the Swan. Alone in the room, he could feel the pastel sun, smell the salt in the air through the rot from debris, almost touch her as she moved, smiled at the camera, waved, her almond eyes bright with life. And in just a week the Swan had been transformed from a derelict hull into a beautiful creature of the sea.

He worried about her now, worried too about unfinished odds and ends on the boat, a loose hatch cover, frayed wiring on the inboard. Why had she given him the holostick—unless she intended to sail away later that morning?

At four a.m. his device screamed its high-pitched alarm, the sharp sound of grief itself. He identified himself to the dispatcher as the Harbors Officer on call with SoCal Red Team.

Yes, he was responsible for Malibu and the coastline to the south. Yet another harbor fire, he was told, coordinates forthcoming. His heart thudded unnaturally in his chest until he heard that he'd be joining Sergeant Rodriguez in turbocopter four.

Then he felt relieved.

Rodriguez worked the San Diego sector exclusively, two hundred clicks south of Long Beach. He never shared Stringer's territory. So if the Army team was going to be led by Rodriguez, they'd be headed down toward the border, to Encinitas or San Diego itself. As for another fire ... statistically, it was overdue.

They put him on a jump jet and he caught the turbocopter at Malibu base, out at the end of the breakwater, just as he had a week before. The actual sight of Rodriguez, plump and muttering to himself as usual, was comforting. Voorst tried to sleep; he'd been able to doze on the jump jet, dreamed a dream of the Swan more vivid than the experience he'd had in the VNN room. But now he couldn't get it back.

Rodriguez shook him awake only minutes out of Malibu.

The column of black smoke was visible from ten clicks away, dense and billowy, shifting in the morning wind like a dye marker in ocean currents.

Photochemical colors in the sunrise sky: mauve and filthy pink. The old Army turbocopter rattled through the airspace above coastal LA descending gradually toward the source of the smoke.

"Hey, where we goin'?" Voorst asked Rodriguez.

"Look for y'self. Long Beach. Don' you guys ever know nothin'?"

"What do you mean, Long Beach. That's Stringer's territory. What would you be doin' going to Long Beach? Where's Stringer?"

"Stringer, the guy's totally fucked and gone, man," Rodriguez laughed against the noise.

Voorst swung up to the open door of the copter's cargo area, one hand on a safety strap, squinting south through the haze at the string of makeshift harbors, the thousands of houseboats and makeshift live-aboards. Now he could see the black cloud rising from Long Beach Harbor all right, from a broad sector of the main channel. A huge vessel was blocking the harbor mouth. The QE 3 was bow down, sinking.

"Jesus. What about Stringer. What do you mean?"

"Jus' look at this," Rodriguez laughed on, punching up a secondary mode on the copter's VNN summary screen. "'S a replay, eight minutes worth. Pix turned up on VNN real-time two hours ago, nobody sayin' how. Jus' look at the asshole."

The first shaky images showed Stringer in a skiff towing a commando float loaded with cases of Lydex.

Someone must have fed illegal footage into the VNN broadcast loop. It was an exposé.

The grainy night shot showed Stringer with his own hands using magnetic grapples to secure the massive charge to rusty plates behind the man-thick anchor chain hanging from the bow of a massive ship. A blue hull. The QE 3.

Stringer dumped fuel from the skiff. Then he fended off, igniting the pilot fire of petrochemicals, turning finally, shock and recognition in his eyes as he saw the camera, the side of his face gruesome, the wrong side of his face bloody in the orange light. His other ear was gone now, his temple stringy with cartilage and slick with gore...

A gaff thrown like a harpoon hit Stringer in the chest as he tried to step away, knocked him to his knees at the gunwale…

In the foreground of the shot, Voorst recognized the deck of the Swan, swarming with blue shirts, the red bowsprit gleaming in the lurid glow.

And he recognized the tanned hand trembling on the tiller, the small bones on the inside of a wrist as delicate as a girl's. The screen showed the Lydex igniting, a sun spinning into a whirlpool of light, bleaching the screen into fine atom snow, a vision of white light so pure that time, for a moment, seemed to stand still.

THE ATCHISON, TOPEKA, & SANTA FE

After a fitful sleep he lay awake in the darkness listening to the house creak, to the furnace cycling. Outside, a heavy snow held the world in silence.

Then a faint spreading gray at the window and something else—down the hall in the living room, where the tree's lights had glowed dimly all night—a movement. When he heard quiet voices for a while, his mother's laugh, he eased himself out of bed—he did not want to be disappointed—and padded into the living room.

And there it was, under the tree, silver track winding through the gifts, the headlight of the streamliner punching out from behind the mountainous tree skirt, its dome car catching red and orange and green lights in frosted windows. He could see from a glance at the open pods among the wrapping paper that his parents had given him the big hybrid set, the one with the state-of-the-art monorail rig, and, more to the point, well, his point, all that retro stuff, starting with the steel streamliner coming his way again. From down at the level of the rug the detail was amazing—you could see little pipes and bolts, springs and couplings on the cars. On the third pass he took in the Santa Fe diesel, a double-ender, like strong jaws back to back, and in its forward cab—he could see a little guy!

He glanced at the packing pod again. Almost everybody else was getting the Mars Habitat thing, you could sit with a holo of astronauts in a Rover, whatever. This one had a

Virtualizer AI chip too, but that wasn't what he'd wanted. He couldn't take his eyes off that train, from its bright headlight through the intertwined fists of the couplers—you could hear the running gear rumble—car by car to the vista dome. When it passed, the track looked like it had been laid over weathered brown ties on tamped tiny gravel. Green tufts grew wheel high in a living miniature world.

He looked up. His dad was beaming. His mom, her hair loose and pretty, had that great smile. "What do you think, kiddo?" she asked.

"It's *perfect,*" Matt said. "Thank you." He looked at his dad with new respect. "It's just what I wanted, exactly what I wanted." So he wasn't going to be punished after all, not for reprogramming the house lights, not for hacking his sister's page. He took in the other pods in the set, the other bright wrappings. "Mom!" he remembered. "I have a present for you."

He was already reaching for the box. In it lay, beautifully folded, the silk nightgown his dad had helped him pick out, all blue and smooth, like water.

He was on the rug again, watching the locomotive coming at him, headlight at eye level. He took in the high cab.

Matt blinked. You *could* see a little guy in there! An engineer! With an engineer's cap and a mustache! You could see his brown eyes! As the train passed by, the little guy waved!

The house smelled like bacon substitute and coffee and hot chocolate. They'd unpacked a mid-sized passenger station, some mining trestles along a spur, and one of those old-fashioned black water tanks. His dad explained about the two-part expanded set, which he already knew, by pulling out a block of suburban-looking houses for the monorail section. Its golden cars matched the futuristic city's curved glass terminal. Time and again as his father unpacked, his attention would drift back to the retro train. It was so cool.

The train looped through his sister's Virtual Field Hockey Tournament, passed his mom, and drove his way again.

"Hey, Dad," Matt observed. "The engineer only waves when he passes by me. Just me."

His dad thought for a bit—he was a professor, ran a busy lab, usually had the answer to anything. "The train's AI locates you through your GPS bracelet," his dad said. Then he grinned. "Part of the upgrade package. You're the registered owner. President of the railroad. He's paying his respects."

His dad knelt to shift a hardware store into position near the old-fashioned passenger station. Power cells kicked in, windows glowed. "When I was a kid," his dad said, "we lived in Grandma Jean's old apartment. I had the world's dinkiest train." He laughed. "Half-HO, all nano. Still, I used to dream about the people in the little houses. I used to dream about a set like this, *three* engines..."

His mom came in, all pretty in blue silk, carrying mugs for each of them.

"Anyway, *this* railroad's for you. The license is in your name. You're going to run a railroad."

After a long day visiting Grandma Jean, his dad was watching the vidwall news in bed. Matt crept out to the tree in his pajamas.

What his dad had said was true. No matter where he lay, the little guy waved at him each time the Santa Fe passed by. The way you could see his expression, his cheeks bunched cheerfully, was amazing.

It occurred to him to stop the train the next time it came by.

When he did so, the little guy waved and shouted, "Hi, Matt."

He'd said his name! "Wait'll I tell my dad," Matt said breathlessly.

"Hang on there, Matthew Pike," the engineer said. "The advanced features of this unit's AI are only available to a single licensed user."

"Oh, right. Only one account." Matt chewed his lip, disappointed he couldn't share the experience with his dad, but thrilled to have the engineer launch into a welcome speech that seemed written especially for him. "And, Matthew Pike?"

the engineer concluded, "Thanks for initializing us. I'm ready to run this EMC-E1 diesel through its paces."

"Uh, anything I'm supposed to do?" Matt asked. That was the question his friend Chris had used to start the setup on his Rover.

"Always keep water in the tank," the engineer said, waving his hand at the old-fashioned high black tank. "We actually use it. We're a wetware AI, Matthew Pike, totally organic."

"We?" Matt said. "There are more of you guys?"

"Welcome aboard," the engineer grinned.

"This is great," Matt said. He could hear his mom putting dishes away. The pictures on the pods merged into his vision of his future layout. When his mom called, he pulled the power cable and started repacking the rolling stock so they could move it downstairs. The little window in the front cab slid closed.

◇

True to his word, his dad got a couple of big pieces of plywood, painted one side green, and set them up on sawhorses in a corner of the basement, under the winter light of the garden window. For a couple of days, his dad worked with his laser saw and driver, framing hills, installing prefab cliffs and tunnels, laying out roads and farms and blocks of buildings from the pods, connecting them by yellow-lined streets with little autos and trucks that were another miracle of realism. The spray-on landscape was organic, only needed periodic misting, you could already see minuscule tendrils of bushes uncurling.

The two boards overlapped to form a wide V. On his left side, by the window, a small modern city took shape beneath the loop of its sleek golden monorail. On his right side, toward the furnace, the Santa Fe's passenger and freight terminal anchored a storefront and bungalow town. Outbound for the Santa Fe was a country village with a covered platform and a church and a square. A stubby steam engine shuttled from the terminal to a mine along the furnace.

Where the boards overlapped, his dad had terraformed a mountain range that divided the lines. From the far side, an excursion spur of monorail pylons swooped up to a flat spot below the far peaks, a meadow, a kind of high-altitude lookout, before it disappeared into a tunnel and back down. The retro railroad's track ran up long switchbacks over trestles and waterfalls to its side of the meadow before a long rocky grade took it down to pastures along the back wall.

What with all the prefab building and landscape units, they were finished in a week. His dad helped him verify the cable runs, power up, and bring each section carefully on line, using the little steam engine as their test vehicle. It was funny—for a while, as he worked, his dad was like a kid, too, you could see it in his face, what he probably looked like when he was a kid.

But just after New Year's, things got busy at the university again and his dad disappeared. "In his lab, like every spring," his mom shrugged, leaving him to run the railroad.

He hadn't logged on to the Mars site Chris had put up in days, even though Chris had loaned him the special headset. There were a lot of little adjustments to make, crossing gates to calibrate, track to align, so much to admire.

When he finally had all the signals installed and picket fences set, he upended the red and silver Santa Fe diesel, pushed the toggle from "demo" to "auto," set its wheels back on the track, coupled it to three passenger cars, then fired it up from his remote. As he did so, the golden monorail slipped by on its pylons against the cliffs in the far background and disappeared into the tunnel.

It was a beautiful dance, the trains moving by and around their curves. There was still something of Christmas in it, a strand of leftover tinsel among the colored lights, evergreen above the meadow. He'd programmed the Santa Fe to run on its long route, switchbacking up the mountains and then back down. On cue the stubby steam engine shuttled down from the mine trestle to bustle around the yard. He parked it under the water tower, and with a little flash of embarrassment realized he had forgotten to fill the tank.

He got a cup of water from the laundry sink. He was watching the Santa Fe on his way back and saw a little movement, the engineer waving at him when the train looped close.

He stopped the Santa Fe on its next pass.

"Hi, Matt!"

He looked carefully at the little guy. He could see lines on his face, his mustache with little curls at the end. The instructions said you could set voice commands by using the engineer to name the file. "Um, what's your name?" he asked.

"Great question. As you've probably figured out, I'm your interface, Matt, the way you communicate directly with your layout using the virtualized AI. Call me Chief!"

Matt took in the tiny engineer, the silver train, the town beyond it, the hills rising, it seemed, miles away. "Awesome," he said. What was the second thing he was supposed to ask? "Chief? Rate this layout."

"Great question. Needs some people."

Matt squinted and looked at the little figure.

"Great question," Chief said again. "Needs some people."

Matt laughed, and sure enough, among the smaller pods, along with a few highly realistic zoo animals, were whole sets of figures—more than a hundred yellow-jacketed ones, the city people with their silver and bronze-uniformed gardeners and security. They had six perfect, tiny cats.

The ten dogs belonged to Chief's world, along with the blue mailman and shoppers and farmers and school kids—at least a hundred more figures. As he set the retro people in place, they seemed more real to him. The monorail city was not for him. It was too generic, too perfect, like the private school he went to, like the Mars Habitat at Chris's, all titanium and polymers and touchscreens, like the holo-ized shows his mom watched.

He let the trains run as he placed the figures. He liked feeling them flex under his fingers, setting them down on sidewalks as the trains danced in the background. The passing windows of the observation car caught his eye. They were opaque, and their blankness troubled him. Was there something else missing?

"Great question," the engineer said. "We could use some food, Matt."

Matt blinked. He hadn't read that far. "Food?"

"Grains of rice. Just fill the mining hopper with grains of rice."

◇

One night in January he crept down the stairs to the basement, halfway down to where the stairs turned and it was shadowy, and from that spot he watched the layout under racing moonlight from the garden window.

It looked like a real place, a countryside seen from far away, from a high glider, perhaps, and he half-dreamed of the sleeping world below under shifting clouds.

Then, all of the railroad's signal lights popped on, tiny red and green lights, and from the now illuminated station the Santa Fe stopped, then reversed to its starting position at the platform. The steam engine pushed its tender slowly beneath the water tank. What the snap?

He thought about it. Obviously the layout was maintaining itself, the equipment keeping itself clean and lubricants distributed. A lot of stuff had those routines. This one was particularly cool.

He wasn't sure when all the lights went off, wasn't even sure how he got to bed, but the next day during geometry it seemed like a dream.

◇

By March he was using a juice pitcher for water and even so he had to fill the tank once a day. And now there were two rice hoppers, his mom had bought a big sack at Walco. As the days passed, the farm crops were peeking up as if they had been watching the calendar, and, as he misted, grass rose higher in the pastures. In the golden city, monorail pylons sported new greenery by a lake alive with paddleboats and canoes. The steam engine had started shuttling flat cars stacked with straw-sized copper pipe into the mine.

One afternoon, as he watched the monorail swing up its long loop on the pylons, the chain of golden cars stopped on its side of the mountain clearing.

That was new, stopping in the middle of a run. How long had it been doing that? To his further surprise, golden doors slid open, and figures with jackets in different shades of yellow moved stiffly out.

Men and women, a girl his age. In their awkward movements was the signature of one overheated robotics chip. Wait till he told Chris.

The driver of the mono stepped off, identifiable by a golden helmet. The driver's movements were smoother, the wave signaling the passengers back into the cars even and natural.

The next day, he brought the Santa Fe up to the pass. He stopped it at the side of the meadow, on its parallel track. Sure enough, the car door swung open, a set of silver steps dropped down, and retro figures moved out, a group of boys, two young women, men in suits. He recognized the family with the dog from figures he had set out at the main terminal! The figures milled around and reboarded one by one. It was awesome.

People had started moving around the retro town, too, he realized, stepping from the store across the street from the station and back, from the firehouse to the diner, little robotic steps.

But when he stopped both trains at the meadow at the same time, all the figures did was mill around beside their cars and then reboard. Time after time, all he got was the same result.

◇

"Hey, kiddo," he heard his mom call across the basement, "how do you start this thing?"

He was at his dad's workbench, lost in sorting out tiny farm equipment—which was the posthole digger? He looked over and there she stood, her blonde hair falling over the shimmering blue shoulders of her robe. She'd wandered over from the laundry. She held the remote in her hand like an empty plate.

The layout was completely dead. Which was funny, because he'd been over there five minutes before, and he had left the lines running on demo routes, low consumption moves that kept the equipment cycling.

Chief had said he loved them.

He had trouble booting up, too. Finally, he did a complete cold reset, but now only the steam engine moved.

The Santa Fe sat at the station like a beautiful museum exhibit. Beyond it children walked stiffly by the firehouse and old men sat on benches by the square. He couldn't remember setting them out. The little town was becoming more populated somehow. So was the city. Finally, the diesels moved.

"Why don't you build a little station up there?" his mom suggested when he told her about the meadow. "Maybe they'll make friends." They talked about school and then both watched the trains' graceful dance, his mom sitting at the far end of the layout, resting her chin in her hands, a dreamy look in her eyes.

It was the Christmas gift of all time. It was so cool.

◇

He turned to his father's workbench again. He started with a platform wide enough to reach both tracks and a shelter. With miniature construction materials from the pod he added an outdoor café with its own deck, a cabin for the owner, and a stable on the retro side.

The figures still just kept by their trains. Over at Chris's, they got into a dust-up with an Aussie Rover—the Mars thing was looking more like a vid game, but it was cool the way it had gone global. Within the week they bumped into a Japanese unit whose probes had been weaponized, and he could barely get a turn.

Then it was Spring Recess and his dad was downstairs saying goodbye before he headed off to the airport for a conference. The night before, his dad had tweaked the robotics chip to run a subroutine that made the animals move.

"Very clever," his dad said. "Very, very clever." His dad was over by the furnace, tracing a run of copper tubing just beneath the vegetation that led to the layout's water tank. The tubing had been routed through the mine from the furnace dehumidifier.

"Jeez," Matt said. "I've been forgetting to fill the tank."

"I guess we can afford the water bill." Matt's dad laughed.

Beyond the diesels standing idle at the roundtable, Chief waved his arm cheerfully back and forth, like a signal. The light shifted, and he saw his mom's legs at the window, among tongues of rising leaves. There was a splatter of dirt and she disappeared.

◇

Passengers from both trains were walking along the meadow platform to the shelter now, sitting in the café. Their motions had become as smooth as wind, couples had formed, and groups of like-sized boys coalesced.

In the retro town, a kneeling figure turned a yard into a thriving garden the next day. Chief walked home from the station at the end of the day to a house with a red door from which spilled a wife and two children. The house had a white fence and a teeter-totter in the back yard made up to look like a steam engine.

The mingling was getting more intense. Over at Chris's, the Japanese had broken his solar array and he was looking for help from the Aussies, but his console had to be sent back for repairs.

◇

Trouble, he saw, *at the meadow.*

The crowd from the retro train had been backed into the shelter by yellow-jacketed passengers from the monorail, pushed into the shelter like trash in a trash can, even though there was plenty of room on the platform behind them.

His hand trembling, he ran undo functions for the monorail and the Santa Fe. The passengers moved back to their cars, and the trains pulled away.

What he hadn't counted on was the Santa Fe leaving a half-dozen passengers behind. He hadn't noticed. They were a family, a mother, father, and three kids. When the monorail looped back up, its passengers swarmed the family. This time it looked ugly, like a fight.

"Chief!" he yelled. Where was the Santa Fe?

Up on the mountain platform, one of the retro figures, the father, had been knocked over. His leg was twisted into an unnatural angle. Matt tried to run another undo function for the monorail line, but the toggle wouldn't engage. More yellow figures were surrounding the fallen father.

"Hi, Matt!" A voice registered from the gingerbread station.

"Chief! Something's wrong. We have an emergency. The layout is acting wrong!"

"Coming up," Chief said grimly.

Chief climbed into the cab of the steam engine in a heartbeat and it was climbing the grade, spewing black smoke and chugging up the trestles.

Up at the meadow platform, the monorail driver had stepped out of the train and moved to the fallen retro figure. The driver knelt on one knee as the yellow-jackets moved away.

Then the driver's helmet rose. Blonde hair spilled over the driver's shoulders.

Matt blinked. The monorail driver was a woman. As she set down her golden helmet and tended to the father, he could clearly see the driver was a young, long-haired woman with a calm, perfect face. In his parents' room, there was a picture of his mother when she was in college, she looked like that.

As the steam engine chugged up the last stretch of track before the meadow, the monorail passengers filed back quickly into their cars. The driver helped the fallen father to his feet—his leg still twisted—and walked back to the lead car. Her door closed just as the steam engine pulled up and the monorail slid away.

His remote was showing a half-dozen error codes.

"Thanks, Chief," Matt said as the engineer stepped down from the cab.

"Kiddo?" his mom called down from the top of the stairs. "Is everything all right down there?"

◇

Even with the trains scheduled to stop at different times, few passengers disembarked at the meadow anymore. His sister teased him. His new snack bar, the platform, the little café, were rather forlorn. He misted the vegetation, adjusted the signals, and tamped the tracks, but that only reminded him of the fight.

That night, he didn't even want to log in to Chris's site. As he lay in bed, he replayed the sight of the monorail driver tucking so much blonde hair back into her helmet, rising from her knees, hand extended to the retro male figure.

"Chief!"

"Hi, Matt."

"Chief, analyze error."

"Simple error," Chief said. "Your new platform is undocumented in setup. The meadow station development is undocumented. It defaults as a lawless place, a no-man's land. Potential bug in the hybrid set? The platform complex needs some rules."

His head spun a bit. Whose fault was that? His? The AI's?

"Security infrastructure options include: a police station, TSI presence, community development sequences," Chief said.

He shut the layout down to its demo routes and headed back to his dad's workbench. The pod of building materials he'd opened was his only hope now.

◇

When he rebooted it was already May. He'd cobbled together a little sheriff's office, a TSI post with surveillance cameras, and manned them with passenger figures from both of the trains. He converted a storefront into a hotel flanked by two cabins to give the place a lived-in feel. Following Chief's instructions, he held off running the trains to the meadow until Saturday afternoon. Chief said he was working at something too.

When he went down to the basement Saturday afternoon, Chief was standing on a little stage at the café end of the platform—where had that come from? Blue and gold bunting surrounded the stage like a skirt.

Then both trains arrived simultaneously at the platform.

Passengers poured out from the trains and formed a crowd before the stage. The monorail driver, shaking her blonde hair out as she removed her helmet, climbed up to stand beside Chief, and they hugged, then raised their hands together. A faint cheer swept down the mountain. Chief delivered a speech Matt couldn't hear, followed by the mono driver. Then they were shaking hands, there was another cheer, and all the figures on the platform began shaking hands, figures in yellow jackets, retro figures in casual clothes, all shaking hands.

The monorail driver, when she faced the crowd—you could see she was so pretty, perfect in her golden jumpsuit, smiling as she raised Chief's arm.

◇

Even Chris was impressed with the layout, though all he wanted to talk about was weaponizing his digging tools when his console came back. He went home early.

Up at the meadow the figures mingled. The trains looped

through their routes and the steam engine shuttled very realistic loads of dirt from the mine. The cars moved and the tractors tilled the country fields. Kids swung on a jungle gym in the schoolyard (very cool). The little world seemed peaceful again.

Then one day he was outside looking for a wooden glider in his mother's small vegetable garden, which was bordered by the plantings outside the basement window. Two yellow-jacketed figures darted out from the end of a lettuce row. At first he couldn't figure out what they were, it was so strange. They disappeared behind the carrots and he traced a path that led to a packed-earth tunnel alongside the foundation. It stopped at the window frame.

On the basement side there was dirt and plant debris on the floor, spattered on the layout. He was shocked. He checked the rice hopper and it was empty. He had neglected the layout lately. It had been running so beautifully.

"Chief!" he yelled as he brought the Santa Fe diesels around. There was no response. To his surprise, in Chief's cab sat the fireman, a mute figure who usually stood stiffly at the controls of the steam engine.

Matt scanned the layout in the late-afternoon light. Chief was nowhere to be found, Matt looked up along the step-faced mountain—it was an hour before trains were scheduled to stop. He searched the empty meadow.

Then he saw them. In the trees, behind the café. Chief was walking with a figure in a gold suit who was holding a helmet. Her blonde hair was spilling over her shoulders. The two figures were holding hands. They passed behind the TSI shed and up the walk to the little hotel, the rustic stone walk he had meticulously laid.

Chief held the door open and followed her in. The door closed behind them like a circuit switching off. Then there was a glow in a rear window.

Matt waited, but they didn't come out.

After dinner, light still glowed in the window. Matt sat at the control console all evening, the layout quiet, staring at his unfinished geometry homework. Near their house by the station, Chief's wife stood beside the picket fence. She was dark-haired, had a round, moon face, like the child who held her at her knees.

Matt tossed and turned in bed. When he slid toward sleep, his mind was filled with her, her train from the perfect city, her blonde hair swirling across her shoulders and down her back, her movements so smooth she seemed made of silk.

◇

Matt was up before breakfast and downstairs even as his mother called from the kitchen that he was going to be late for school.

He found Chief dozing in the diesel's cab at the gingerbread station.

"I don't think the AI is supposed to do stuff like that," Matt said thickly.

Chief was not smiling. He looked older and mean. Chief gazed around the terminal before he looked directly at Matt. "It's you," Chief said with a leer. "The AI is configured on you. It's your imagination, Matthew Pike."

◇

He couldn't concentrate in English. When he got home that afternoon, there was a crowd at the monorail terminal. There were more children than he'd ever seen, ten times as many as he'd put out. Little mounds of earth surrounded the bases of trees flanking the suburban stop. Tiny green fruit hung at the ends of the branches.

His face flushed. His hand shook as he reached for and tripped the main power switch for the console.

A yellow light flashed on his panel. His dialogue bar blinked: DO NOT DISCONNECT.

Matt keyed in the command for a cold boot. He waited, but the kill command just triggered a backup.

The monorail moved along the back of the layout,

swinging around its golden loop on the far side of the modern city, all right angles and trees in planters. The steam engine shuttled loads of dirt from the mine.

◇

His mother complained that he wasn't paying attention, but he was. The Kennedys were going to drop off his father from the airport.

He went downstairs after dinner.

"Chief!"

"Hi, Matt!" Chief leaned out of the red and silver cab of the Santa Fe.

"Chief, I'm going to tell my dad. I want to shut down the layout."

"Security alert, Matthew Pike. Backup has engaged to save what you have created. To shut the line down with the main breaker will terminate the landscape, the plants and the animals, and all the new people. It will destroy this little world."

"I want this to stop."

"When you want to start up again, some of your initialization materials will have been compromised, and the manufacturer cannot guarantee that the trains will operate. That's what we're trying to avoid. But if that's what the license holder wants..."

"Hi, Matt!" a woman's voice called out.

Chief's wife walked beneath the cab window. "We can work it out, Matthew Pike," she said. "That's what we like about you. When you see something wrong, you fix it, Matthew. You fixed the meadow. You stopped the fighting."

True. It was really a cool present, after all. "I did. I made new buildings, and..." Now he saw two figures on the floor, a tiny ladder on the cable run.

"So you don't really have to worry," she said, comfort in her voice.

"I just want a railroad," he said. "A model railroad."

"Consider it done," Chief said.

"So first, everybody stays on the layout."

"Done." The figures on the floor moved up clever little steps on the sawhorse.

"See?" Chief's wife said. "You can make it work. The AI is you, Matthew Pike."

But the next night he crossed the backyard to run the trash out behind the garage. Somebody had left the door open, and when he went in to close it on his way back, he took in the smell of rubber and batteries and the sight of his mom's Subaru, its thick cable feed resting on the floor. A movement caught his eye. Along the stud above the outlet he counted five of the figures moving along like a centipede. Up in the corner, he saw a half-dozen more.

"Matt?" his mother asked as the sliding door thumped behind him. "Have you been in my closet?"

◇

He slept fitfully.

He was up at first light. He should have known better.

His father had come home late and his parents were still sleeping.

When he got some juice, he saw figures by the back door. There were two in the kitchen cabinet. The little figures were all over the house now, like ants.

He went downstairs and looked. The layout seemed healthy, green and colorful, but he couldn't see any people.

He studied the place, a lovely little world with its square fields, farm trucks on the roads, tiny boats at a dock on the monorail lake. As he scanned the retro town, a color caught his eye.

Hanging on the line outside the cottage was a blue piece of silk.

"Hi, Matt!" A stranger in a gold jacket spoke to him from the cab of the Santa Fe.

"I'm telling my dad. I'm telling him now."

"Matt!"

But he had already turned away. He was climbing the

stairs. Then at the head of the stairs, he saw the crowd of figures. He would have to step on them to pass by.

He ran back down the stairs, slipping off his GPS bracelet. He pushed it into the tool drawer of his father's workbench.

When they had gathered by the workbench, he tiptoed past and up the stairs.

"Dad!" he yelled. He heard a voice, his mom's. He pushed open the door of their bedroom.

◇

His parents were bound by fishing line in the bed, swarmed by the tiny figures. The shock was numbing, like he'd been hit by a car.

His mother looked at him from her pillow with a wan smile. "Hey, kiddo," she said. "Can you help us out here?"

He was transfixed by the pattern of fishing line that bound her to the bed. It began at her shoulders, crisscrossing down to her ankles, passing beneath her arms and between her breasts, like a web across her stomach and hips outlined beneath the sheet. His father had been gagged, trussed in the fetal position, and wrapped in a blanket, utterly helpless. Maybe the main breaker, Matt thought. Maybe if he pulled the main breaker for the house?

"*Kiddo*?"

"Mom! Dad!"

He was twisting, tumbling, falling.

The cold oak floor was hard against his burning cheek.

THE LIGHTS

As usual the strobe lights were making his eyes water. He was sitting in the rec pod, fighting off an incipient migraine, watching the free dancing and trying to come to terms with what Miika had done to her hair. That's when the announcement came over the ship's intercom. He blinked to adjust to the normal illumination.

"Our long-range probes have registered coherent energy patterns, possible alien forms on the second planet from sun A5848," Captain Blake was saying, annoyance clipping his words. "Even a transport like us is required to investigate. I regret the delay as much as all you farmers will, and I regret even more ..." – Blake's sigh of disgust was an audible rush – "that without regular scientific crew my orders are to put this ship into an orbit around the planet, and to send a shuttle down to investigate with whatever research-certified personnel..."

With the word "delay," Jackson's attention had drifted back to Miika again. She was standing, hip cocked, bouncing slightly to the beat she was keeping in her mind, her shiny bald head swinging from side to side. She had shaved off all of her hair! He had been attracted to her in the first place because of the lush thickness of her tresses, and now they were gone. None of the rest of the women had been affected by the fashion show from Ganymede Colony, the agro planet to which they were being transported, but she'd bought everything on the menu, the silver fingernails, the silver lipstick, the shaved head. Why were beautiful women so shallow? He'd even liked the faint shadow of hair above her upper lip—gone now. If he weren't too shy and awkward to free dance himself...

He was startled by the sound of his own name over the intercom. Everyone in the lounge was looking at him, even Miika, whose eyes had gone wide. The Captain had signed off and now Miika was coming over. Jackson was left with the incomprehensible reverberation of his own name in his head.

"... of all people," Miika said, smiling warmly, putting her hand on his.

"I didn't hear what Captain Blake was, uh, talking about," he said shamefacedly. "I don't, uh..."

"They're sending a team down on a shuttle to that planet they're getting signals from. You're fourth man on the landing party. Nobody's ever been on that planet before. How utterly..."

"Me?"

"You're research-certified," she said. "You're about the only one."

His heart sank. Now here was something else for him to screw up on the voyage. He was a specialist only in plant diseases. He'd never even been in a download suit before. The music was starting up again and the strobe started to flash.

"How supra exciting. Wanna free dance?"

When he stood up Jackson could see the slight slick sheen on her dome, the dizzying invitation in her eyes. She was wearing silver-tinted contacts. He hung his head and rubbed his throbbing temples. "I better go study up on a download suit," he muttered miserably. "I don't wanna go down there and die."

◇

"Listen," Captain Blake was saying, scratching the blonde stubble on his chin, "in years of looking, no alien life form bigger or smarter than a dog's been verified, so let's not get excited, right? Jackson? I'm talking to you."

Jackson bounced down in the zero-grav of the shuttle,

waving his arms for balance. "Just getting used to the suit, sir. I thought it would be, uh, cumbersome."

"Well, there's atmosphere down there, so we're not using helmets. Just make sure you use the O_2 supplements. And leave all but one of those specimen cases behind. We're not going to stay on the surface a minute longer than the twelve-hour minimum, do you all understand that? I want to get to Ganymede on time and get all those damned farm animals out of my pressurized hold."

Jackson thought he saw the veterinarian who had been conscripted along with him glower, but the Flight Vane Engineer nodded grimly. Before they cut loose, the engineer laid out the data again: the probes had picked up coherent light, patterns which fit the language protocol, multiple moving sources. "So the protocol triggered this looksee," he said, barely a flicker of interest in his eyes. "You ask me, an' I told the Captain, we're gonna find some weather phenom and a bug in the protocol program."

Just when Jackson thought he had it—his arms one way, his legs another, his trunk in rhythm—if it wasn't exactly a free dance it might pass for one—Captain Blake slapped the thruster control with the palm of his hand, Jackson's stomach turned a loop, and he hung on for dear life.

The plain upon which they had landed was dun-colored, rocky, cut by low arroyos formed by erosion, though it was obvious to Jackson that any water had evaporated off the surface of the planet thousands of years before. The clouds were high, pink, wispy. Jackson sucked on his supplemental oxygen tube contemplatively, gazing at the bleak landscape, the line of red bluffs in the distance, considering how he was going to describe the surface to Miika when he got back.

The Flight Vane Engineer had set up the portable computer on its tripod and was fiddling with the probes distractedly, trying to avoid the wrath of Captain Blake, who paced hands on hips, a dark look on his face. A fat reddish sun hung in the sky.

"I don't see any coherent light," Blake muttered. "I told you to put us right in the middle of the set. I don't see a goddamned thing."

"That *is* where I put us," the Flight Vane Engineer said, looking into the steel cone of one of the probes so intently it seemed as if he wanted to crawl inside and hide.

"Well, find something," Blake said, waving his arms, glaring at the men.

Jackson hurried back to the specimen rack he'd set next to the shuttle and shoveled tiny piles of dust onto the trays. The automatic analyzer signified that the dust was, in fact, ferrous oxide, basalt particulates, carbon particles, a hint of quartz. In summary, it was dust. The carbon was promising but electron micro showed no spores, bacteria, virus. No life.

"I don't see any trace of animal life," the vet told Captain Blake after a short hike around the area. "Except maybe for you, ho ho." He took a swig from a brown unlabeled bottle and politely burped. "Maybe those lights were electrostatic charges in the atmosphere after all." He leaned back against the starboard landing pontoon, patting it first to make sure that it had cooled, and raised his bottle to his lips again.

"Electrostatic charges. We come all this way to look at the weather," Captain Blake grumbled. "What the hell are you drinking?"

The veterinarian took the bottle from his lips, held it away from his body and looked at it with a slightly stunned innocence. "I'm, er, sorry, sir. It's a little home brew from the farmer's co-op. It's beer."

The Flight Vane Engineer looked up from a tangle of wires beneath his tripod. "I hope you've got more."

"As a matter of fact..."

Jackson saw the bright flashes first: beyond the bluffs, resolving into narrow beams. They spit out a sequence, like a code, then repeated. There were a dozen of them. For a brief moment they reminded Jackson of the strobe lights which illuminated Miika's free dancing, then they were gone.

"Good eyes, Jackson," the vet said, saluting him with a raised bottle.

"We'd better move up there," the Flight Vane Engineer told the Captain.

"This time put us on the right spot."

◇

They had to go through a whole launch rigmarole to get the shuttle up into the bluffs. Jackson watched from the rear port: although the planet seemed to be basically a desert, the bluffs, the ridge-backed mountains beyond, were really very dramatic. They clunked down on a flat spot right where he'd seen the lights, right near the edge, with a dizzying view of the plain. But no sooner had they landed than they saw the lights again, this time from a high plateau in the direction of sunset. Captain Blake quickly took his own fix on the spot, determined the source to be stationary at least while transmitting, and decided they should move again. At the third site there was enough level ground to keep Jackson's knees from knocking as he hiked around gathering soil samples for his specimen trays. But there was no other evidence that the precise spot was fundamentally any different from the gritty soil a thousand meters away.

"Though I'm, uh, finding more quartz, sir, and some mica. Maybe those lights emanate from mineral harmonics somehow. Say some grav or mag pattern sets up a current."

The Flight Vane Engineer, tangled up with his wires under the tripod again, knocked over his beer bottle, already empty. "So where's the complex pattern come from?"

"Could be produced by the crystal structure," Jackson suggested. The vet toasted his hypothesis by raising his third bottle of beer, and Jackson took a deep, satisfied breath. Between the slightly reduced gravity of the planet, the crisp atmosphere of the plateau, and the exhilarating landscape, he felt terrific. "Or the process could have produced a form of life—I mean the light itself could have evolved into a form of life, it's possible, and maybe these different geological features..."

"You've been sucking too much supplemental oxygen," Captain Blake said. "Look, you've got the end of your tube all chewed up."

"Sir?"

Blake and the others followed the focus of Jackson's widening eyes, the specimen shovel pointed back toward the plain.

There they were again, brilliant points of light stretching into intense beams, sputtering out a strobe-like sequence of impressive complexity. The Flight Vane Engineer got a probe turned around, and when the lights shut down he took a long pull on another beer, dribbling a bit down his chin because he was keeping his eyes on his computer's read-out screen.

"Different signal set entirely, Captain," he said. "But it fits, I'll be damned, the same language protocol."

Blake groaned and banged the ship with his fist. He squinted up at the fat red sun, shimmering and huge now that it was so low in the sky. The landscape was turning deep purple, rare shades of scarlet and ochre, the plain striped with almost theatrical shadows. "All right," Blake said. "We're staying here through the planet's night. Right here. Veterinary officer, break out that second case of beer. There's some bedding under the aft deck."

"Sir?"

"What now, Jackson?"

"Do you mind if I sleep outside?" Bright stars were already visible rising on the far horizon, opposite the setting sun. "It would be like, um, camping."

"I don't care what you do. But I'm telling you all this: unless we turn up something firm, we're taking the data we have and hauling out of here at sunrise. Let somebody else figure it out. I want to make my schedule. I will make my schedule for transport. Understand?"

The vet passed Jackson an open bottle of beer—a dark

malt, and very strong. The first swig alone seemed to give him a headache. He set the bottle down and went to fish out a bedroll.

◇

Only when the sun had fully set did he realize just how bright the stars were—but of course, he thought, gazing upward into the neon twinkle: thin atmosphere, thousands of near suns. There had been no emanations since the last sighting from the plain, and the rest of the crew had polished off what turned out to be a total of three cases of strong beer. Now, hours later, they slept snoring in the shuttle cabin, and Jackson lay on his back, still looking up—it seemed impossible to him that there wasn't intelligent life somewhere—rehearsing some casual way in which he could mention to Miika that he had camped out all alone, braving the unknown.

Again he shut his eyes and tried to sleep. He went over the long day in his crowded mind, could feel the weariness deep in his bones, but soon his legs twitched and his eyes came open again. The sight of the vast dome of the heavens above him, lying as he was among the tiny function lights of the probes the Flight Vane Engineer had set out, made him feel suspended in a sea of illuminated jewels. A constellation of blue-white stars directly overhead seemed curiously like the arrays of lights they had seen. They winked rhythmically and reminded him of the strobe lights in the rec pod—and Miika danced into his mind again, her silver shape frozen in time with the music, her breathtaking womancurves, her silver eyes. Miika: the perfect slick dome of her head, her attractively thick lips disfigured by silver lipstick, the marvelous sight of her hips and thighs as she brought her arms back and across, a free dancing angel.

When he tried to think about something else he could feel every tiny rock he had failed to clear from beneath his bedding. He sat up and clicked on the emergency light he'd brought along, flashing it momentarily on the shuttle to make certain it was still there.

He decided to slip out of his bedroll and walk around. Once he had stretched and taken a few steps in the brisk atmosphere, his body seemed to tingle and he stopped, setting his arms out wide. In the deep blue void beyond, the air seemed charged somehow, slightly incandescent. Who would see him here? Legs this way, arms that way—yes, that was it, more or less. He rocked his head, his trunk, took the steps again, free dancing, the cone of illumination from his flashlight playing over the mountains in a dizzying rhythm. It wasn't quite right, his rhythm, but he tried, tried again.

Then it was as if the cosmos had exploded, with him at the center.

Jackson was overcome by a brilliance so great he thought for a moment he had been atomized, but no, he could see his feet, his still dancing feet, colors all around him, through him, in him: yellows and reds and greens and blues of such purity and intensity that he would have fallen to his knees overwhelmed had not a new energy filled him as well, an electricity that seemed to penetrate his spine and discharge in each of his nerve cells. It was wonderful! He was feeling, even as he was thinking all colors are contained in white, and the lights screamed all around him. The rhythm he had been trying to find in his head was in the lights now, it was extraordinary. The light, the rhythm, was in his arms too, his legs, his fingers, his toes—it seemed to penetrate into the very cells of his muscles and nerves, he was the dancer and the dance. It was as if new electric blood surged through his heart, and he danced, danced, danced.

The experience seemed to last for hours. He found himself finally a hundred meters away from his bedroll, standing with the single beam of his emergency light shooting off into the darkness. It still moved, ever so slightly, to the new rhythm in his mind, and he felt utterly grand, a new man, excited and transformed.

He ran back to the ship and banged on the hatch. "Captain Blake! The lights, the lights!"

He had to bang away for a full three minutes. Finally, the

hatch popped open and the Captain swayed woozily into the hatchway, his flight uniform rumpled, his hair awry, one eye closed. Even from three meters away, Jackson caught the sour odor of his breath. Captain Blake held his head in his hands, groaning.

"Sir, I've seen the lights again."

"Jackson, you scum," Captain Blake croaked, "if you bother me before daybreak, I'll … I'll have you executed."

"But sir … the lights, they were right here."

"Probes," he heard the Flight Vane Engineer mumble behind the Captain. "… 'as why probes. Cannu unnerstan'?"

Jackson squeezed his eyes shut in frustration and found he could still see the lights with crystalline clarity, a miraculous rainbow of pink and lime and orange. He snapped his eyes open. "Sir, you don't under…"

"*Ex*-ecuted," Captain Blake cut him off. "It's my right." And then the Captain slammed the hatch shut with a clang.

At first it frightened him that he could call the lights back when he closed his eyes, but it wasn't hard to get used to the new rhythm in his bones, the new bounce to his step. He considered recording some notes on his specimen analyzer, but he free danced for a while again. He could swear his coordination had improved, that his nervous system was responding to some new intelligence. When he lay back down on his bedroll an hour later, wondering if he was too excited to sleep, another wonderful thing happened: the lights in his mind turned pastel, dimmed as if in consideration, and he fell immediately into a deep, sound slumber, the kind of sleep he hadn't had since he'd been hiking to collect new plant diseases as a graduate student.

The crew didn't emerge from the shuttle until three hours after sunrise, Captain Blake's face ashen, the Flight Vane Engineer with his T-shirt on backwards, the vet stumbling down the ladder and sprawling cursing in the dust. For a full ten minutes the men communicated in a variety of debauched moans, relieved only when the vet found one last brown bottle and popped it open with a spasm of his wrist.

"A dop, I meana drop, of the fuel that launched 'ya. Thassa only cure," he said.

"I'm telling you, Captain," Jackson said, "the lights became a part of me. Not ten meters from my bedroll."

"Had to be drunker than the rest of us," Blake growled. "You oughta leave that stuff alone. An' stop shouting."

"But sir, if you just check the probes, you'll see..." He wasn't shouting and what was strange too was the new confidence he felt. He'd had an inkling of it early that morning when he'd walked to the edge of the cliff and hadn't been afraid in the slightest.

His explanation was cut short by the Flight Vane Engineer's rapid cursing: he'd caught one of the probe leads in the moon boots he'd been securing and knocked the computer off its tripod. Jackson felt sorry for the man, then embarrassed for him when it turned out that he had connected two of the probes to the wrong inputs before turning in the night before. "Think 'is Jackson did it," the Flight Vane Engineer tried to maintain, but the Captain pointed out that the engineer had drunk half a case himself before he'd set the probes. Then he demanded the partial data.

"Issinany," the Flight Vane Engineer muttered.

"What?"

"Isn't any," the Flight Vane Engineer spit out. "An' don't shout, please. Tol' you two probes wrong. Crashed alla data."

Captain Blake laughed wildly, hysterically. "No data? No data?" Then he abruptly shook his head, his expression flat, and glared at Jackson. "You were hallucinating. That's what you saw, hallucinations. You drank too much."

"No I didn't and I wasn't hallucinating. The lights were right here."

"Garrg," Blake choked. "Whata we gonna... What time is it?" He tried to focus on his device, but he'd strapped it on upside-down, then he looked up at the huge red sun, already thirty degrees high. The shock of the bright light brought his hands up over his eyes. "Jesus, wonner if I can fly."

"But..."

"Gotta. Behind already." He brought his hands down. His eyes were bleary but the resolution in them was unmistakable. "All of you: forget what's happened here. Wipe it from your minds. We're packing it in, unnerstan' me? We got a schedule to make. I don' want you sayin' a word about what happened here or all our asses are cooked."

"Please don' shout," the vet pleaded.

Jackson looked frantically over the plain for a sign of light, but he saw only the dun-colored desert, not a twinkle.

The lights were there only when he closed his eyes.

There was a plant he'd seen once, while doing his graduate research in plant pathology, not a diseased plant but a diphrangium with star-shaped blossoms whose beauty had taken his breath away. Even though Miika looked a little funny now—she was wearing a cap to hide the stubble until her hair grew completely back, and her eyebrows looked like tiny hedges—she gave him the same feeling those star-shaped blossoms had, an awe at the delicacy of the shape he beheld, a liquid weakness at his knees, an unwillingness to blink lest the sight of her disappear in the instant. She led him over to the large port at the end of the rec pod where other lovers were watching Ganymede grow as they approached, a blue-white world of swirling clouds. The second planet from sun A5848, the planet the research team had briefly explored, was two weeks behind them.

"You make my toes tingle just to watch you *walk* now," Miika whispered. "And when you dance! Even the other girls tingle all over. Jackson, I'd do anything for you." She self-consciously picked at the last remaining trace of silver polish on her little finger. "I look so ugly. But when my hair does grow back..."

"You'll be even more beautiful than you are now," he smiled.

"You're so nice. The best free dancer on the ship. I'm so in love with you."

"And I'd do anything for you, too."

She gazed at the growing planet for a long moment, the fertile globe where they would be spending the rest of their lives together. "Will you tell me what really happened back there? You know, when those lights started flashing at the ship, all the farm animals started rutting."

"The data's supposed to be, um, classified," he said, but when she leaned against him and he felt the warmth of her body, he knew he was going to be indiscreet.

"Did the team find a new form of life? Did you communicate with it?"

"Yes, I think so."

"What did it say?"

"Nothing really. It was light, light itself."

"Oh, Jackson."

"Still, I think it was friendly."

She giggled. "All right," she said. "I won't bother you about it anymore. Just so you kiss me at least once every day for the next fifty years. I can't believe I see stars when you do. Stars and rainbows and flashes of color—I thought they just made that up. Nobody ever told me it would really be like this."

TRAFFIC

> He must go by another way who would escape
> this wilderness, for that mad beast that fleers
> before you there, suffers no man to pass.
> She tracks down all, kills all, and knows no glut,
> but, feeding, she grows hungrier than she was.
>
> – *Dante, Inferno I*

What follows, like a snaking line of cars, is the story of the first time I ever set foot inside a Nomad vehicle. It was one of those days: traffic was a bitch.

I was late for my analyst's, and the usual ground-level routes through Studio City were tangled by buses and vans. The sidewalks along Moorpark were either stacked with illegal parking or in use as right turn lanes. I was creeping along in my Jupiter, an old electric bomb, behind a silver Benz, a replica diesel; the Benz belched black smoke so dense I didn't notice the gridlock at Coldwater until I was part of it. I backed through an alley only to find my path obstructed by an articulated trash hauler so huge, so sinister, I thought of Dante at the beginning of the Commedia, his way blocked by the she-wolf of appetite. And then, approaching the gridlock at Coldwater again via the drive-through lane of the Marcos Whiplash Clinic, I saw in the fluorescent blue haze blanketing the intersection a vision from Hell itself: out of the sea of traffic a red intake port began to surface, snoutlike, lupine. The glistening black pickup on whose hood it was mounted was customized with enormous soft tires twice the height of a man. Sounding an airhorn, it surged forward mightily, first bumping the Lexus ahead, then climbing the slope of its trunk and the Hyundai's in the next lane, cresting over both cabins, bumping, gyrating, crushing its way forward.

Then it turned in my direction.

Only in LA, I told myself, could it come to this.

So I swung through the telltale camp of shabby cardboard huts, the Nomad camp everybody was pretending not to see. I blew my horn, scattering two poor Nomad families in their earth-colored rags, then punched through to one of the abandoned ramps of what used to be called the Ventura Freeway. I was trying, as you may have guessed, to bypass the Coldwater mess by getting on a Nomad Interface, a section of urban roadway Nomads are permitted to cruise when they drop down off the Interstate, what they call The Way.

Usually Residents like me, even Residents like the madman in the truck, avoid the Nomad Interface. I had a pirated ambulance chip mounted on my firewall to get me through even undocumented barriers like this one—without the chip, of course, you fry. At the end of the trash-strewn lane of crumbling concrete I felt my old Jupiter vibrate through the electronic membrane. I merged onto the Ventura as if I belonged there.

On the Interface, the right lanes were thick with Nomad loadcarriers uncoupling on the fly. If the drivers ever stop, as everyone knows, they forfeit their rigs and wind up in cardboard shacks like those I'd driven through. Transfer cabs licensed to switch the loads to and from the city zipped around the middle lanes like house lizards in a world of brontosaurial thirty-two and sixty-four wheelers. I finally got up to speed on the viaduct over Sepulveda Boulevard.

That's when my Jupiter—with a sickening whump and sizzle from the front end—lost power.

I coasted onto the shoulder and made some calls on my cell. Under the hood I found my SunStar system and batteries fused into a blackened blob of polycarbon and ceramics. I couldn't even find the socket for my chip.

Then the sirens went off, the ones in the membrane, the ones that announce the daily clearing of all Nomads' vehicles from the Interface. A fine time for this, I remember thinking; you need a chip even to walk off.

That's when I saw the Nomad rig, a white forty footer, creeping my way on the shoulder. A boy wearing an EARTHQUAKE '48 cap was leaning out, his hand on the door handle as the rig loomed toward me. "Hey Mister," the kid yelled—I could see an old guy driving, his white hair long in the Nomad way—"you wanna upload?"

The sirens were wailing. Back a click down at the foot of the viaduct, Jurassic earth-moving equipment was already clearing the stragglers.

I'd never been so close to a Nomad vehicle before. I put my driving shoe on the brass footplate, grabbed the carved handhold, and swung through the open door.

◇

The cab I tumbled into was dim with muted colors. My new silver suit, trendy in LA, made me feel immediately self-conscious. I took a deep breath and almost gagged: organic fabrics, leather, grease, food, fossil fuels, and … what else? Was it true that Nomads never bathed?

"Hey!" the old guy yelled above the high-frequency wail. "You understand? We're headed up the ramp."

Now the hair rose on the back of my neck. As the old guy'd said, the big I-5 ramp, the ramp out of LA, loomed in the tinted windshield. The Nomad swarm of vehicles funneled its way, glimmering under their diesel stacks and solar arrays. In the dusty red light a few illegal peds dodged police APCs, running for the shoulder, scattering along the membrane like it was the southern border, getting jolted: *ash in a flash*, as they say on the street. I started a quick inventory of my life but never got past the problems I was going to talk to my analyst about: tension at the architectural firm where I work, and my rocky engagement to Denise, a woman obsessed with parking spaces. Maybe what I needed was a short adventure.

"Boy, is my mom gonna flame when she finds out we loaded a porker," the kid said. "I mean a parker. Sorry."

"I fused my chip," I told the old guy. "I don't know what to do."

"Then ride with us, stranger. There're places we can get you back across. There's Hubbard's Cave in Chicago."

"Chicago?"

We approached the abandoned toll booths. They marked a kind of border: to the east lay the Interstate, true Nomad territory, disappearing into land darkening as with a change of weather.

Looking into the vast black heart of it, I swooned.

◇

When I woke the next morning, I found myself in a bunk aft in the vehicle, a small patch of UV glass beside me, the creosote scrub of Nevada stretching to the horizon. The truth was, it was sublime. A range of mountains stood clearly in the distance, purple and clean. The electronic fence that kept the Nomads on the road and off the land was barely visible as a series of thin towers. Horrible though my dislocation was, I could see what the Nomads liked about their way of life: the space, the steady movement, the low-level atmosphere you could see right through.

And out there, well, traffic wasn't that bad. The big rigs—the stupendously oversize vans, the double-wide trailers, the canvas-flapping Omars, the sedans, the commercial flatbeds—all moved like a herd of animals, in an orderly, coordinated way, our speed about as fast as a person can run.

Up forward, a graceful woman in her late twenties was driving. She wore the big Nomad earrings, the oversize tunic and chaps, the muted colors. She turned out to be the boy's mother, Acura. I felt self-conscious about my silver suit again; when the light hit the fabric the right way, it actually reflected its surroundings.

I eased myself into the passenger's seat with an ingratiating smile. Acura was attractive, even smelled good, spicy and floral at the same time.

I suppose I was a little intoxicated by her. Or disoriented by the experience of continuous motion. "Isn't it maddening not to stop?" I blurted out, trying to be friendly. "I've always felt you people had a right..."

Her ice-blue eyes narrowed. "You people?"

"I'm sorry. I mean, um, you ... folk."

"Us folk? Just where are *us folk* supposed to demand our rights?" she asked, her lips tight. "Just where?"

She was technically correct about the Nomad human rights problem.

Nomad life first began, I remember reading, when the refinement of low-v solar rigs coincided with a movement among long-haul truckers to stay on the road all the time. In the cities, mobile offices had already hit the road in the shape of customized supervans, "transient architectural mechanisms," wrote *Newsweek*, spawned by roads so choked that cities like LA or Bangkok took days to cross. During the housing crisis of '37, commuters with long drives and low budgets abandoned their mortgages and started living full-time in enhanced RV's, joining the thousands of Sioux and Arapaho on the Interstate who'd gone on trek in Winnebagos. The traffic, as they say, merged. Intermarried. When children were born on the road, Nomad Nation became history.

The downside was that native born, "indigenous" Nomads had no legal residence. Their disenfranchisement remained starkly visible: if Nomads got past the membrane, they were relegated to cardboard shacks on deserted freeway ramps. They joined those who'd stopped, the lot of them illegal immigrants unable to qualify even for survival welfare.

"I'm sorry," I said, "I was just..."

"You're just lucky I was sleeping when they saw you."

"I was in trouble."

"I would have never let them pick you up," she said,

a vein throbbing on her forehead. "What were you doing out there, anyway? Taking a short-cut? You parasite."

"The sirens went off," I said sullenly. True, the problems I'd been driving to discuss with my analyst, particularly the problems at work, seemed trivial now. "They would have just scraped me into the Interface."

"All Ryder could talk about this morning was how we had a porker on board."

"The kid? His name's Ryder?"

"You just leave him alone."

Her anger made me ashamed. These nice people, I thought, could wind up living on an off-ramp. "I'll get out of your way as soon as I can," I said.

She turned to me as if to say something, but my suit had gone reflective and she started looking at me as if I was some idiot who'd become partially transparent. I felt a hand on my shoulder. "Hubbard's Cave," the old man, Mack, said. I could see Ryder behind him, rubbing his eyes.

Alongside us Nomad traffic moved as relentlessly as a big ocean swell.

◇

All the Resident news media—CNN, VNN, ABC—paint a picture of the Nomads as gypsy truckers, as transients with cattle trailers, as assorted other road trash. But I saw a different world out there on the Twenty Lane Trail.

To begin with, at the heart of the swarm aren't transport herds but fleets of caravans driving clustered around mobile shops and services to make up moving communities. I saw curtains in windows, kitchen gardens under sliding skylights. Around noon we passed Nomads eating in a self-propelled restaurant, retro-styled as a railroad dining car, its power panels hidden in the silver of its roof. A long doublewide functioned as a repair center; your rig was raised into it like a dry dock. One supervan turned out to be a veterinary clinic (one out of every four Nomads towed animals). All the facilities were compact, and I'd guess you'd have to say, primitive, but there was a beauty to them, to the funky efficiency of wood and mylar docking ports.

That day I stuck to my compartment, ate lunch alone, staring out the window, eventually watching the light fade over the traffic and Utah. Ryder came by and invited me to dinner with him and his Granddad at a Nomad "Campfire" — we'd have to step over to a moving flatbed. Mack was behind him, said it was OK, a place kids went to hang out, that I should see more of Nomad life.

I got up and stretched. "I'd love to," I said.

"You can't go like that," Ryder said, waving his hand at my shiny clothes.

"This is all I have."

Mack studied me for a long moment. "We've got some men's clothes in the back," he said.

He did indeed: from a locker beyond the galley, he pulled oversize Japanese trousers, an organic fiber shirt, and a soft jacket, a nice one, of burgundy leather.

I saw the woman, Acura, briefly, just as Mack docked our rig, a moment before Ryder and I stepped over. I'd been obsessed with her ice-blue eyes all day, her sharp intelligence. Now her wavy brunette hair was loose around her shoulders. I thought she might smile with some sort of approval when she saw the earth tones of my borrowed clothes. But she only seemed startled when she saw me. Then she wouldn't meet my eyes.

The encounter left me slightly shaken for reasons I couldn't explain. I crossed nervously to a huge flatbed at the center of which burned an artificial fire of used railroad ties. There was a crowd, which took some getting used to — lots of teens, some of them couples, some of them chaperoned by their parents, older people, babies in cloth carriers, a Sioux chief in full regalia, a group of musicians. Dinner was a blur of wholesome simple food on non-slip plates. Afterwards there was singing, long simple chords and the warble of women's voices. The company confirmed for me a sense that all of life was here on the road.

◇

Acura's eyes had a dark quality, as if she'd been crying, when I joined her up front after we'd reboarded. I couldn't think of anything to say. Then Mack stepped up to spell her at the wheel just as I was slipping off the burgundy jacket.

In a flash I realized whose clothes I'd been wearing: the jacket in my hands was much too big for Mack. The trousers, the coat, the shirt, they belonged to Acura's husband.

As tactfully as I could, I asked about him.

"Why don't you tell us?" Acura said bitterly. "Tell us about Kill a Nomad Day. Tell us about hospitals that have to keep moving. Tell us about living in cardboard teepees." She pushed past me and disappeared into the back of the rig.

Mack looked at me after he adjusted the rearview mirrors. He nodded for me to stay in the passenger's seat.

"He was shot by Residents?" I asked Mack.

He shook his head. "Wasn't that. We had to leave him at the Mayo Exit, up on the I-94 in Minnesota. They sometimes help our kind—but they didn't help Chevy." His son-in-law, he explained, had died of kidney problems well beyond the capabilities of Nomad clinics. Chevy's entry into a Resident medical center had been denied. The chance for help had meant abandoning him, but the help had not come.

Now I felt stupid again, really stupid. "It was very generous of you to let me board," I said.

The next day I kept out of Acura's way, out of respect. I played checkers with Ryder and watched the landscape of Wyoming slide by a streaked side window as if the white light mountains themselves were on the move. Then came the interminable rolling plains of Nebraska and Iowa.

We crossed the Mississippi, gliding over a silver arch, and entered Illinois.

I'd put myself in the front seat beside Acura again, determined to part with her on good terms.

"So it'll be goodbye," I said.

"And good riddance."

"Look," I said. "I've apologized as best I can for what happened to your husband. I don't know what else I can do. I didn't make the world the way it is. Give me a break, OK?"

"We're just different," she said. "I mean Nomads and Residents. We're different kinds of people."

"I'm not sure that's what I've been seeing."

"Then you haven't seen straight. Nomads don't turn people away and Nomads don't collect so much baggage in their lives they can't even move—like lead-walled holo rooms just to play satellite-link teledildonics. We don't leave scars on the earth wherever we go. We don't leave anything."

"Maybe some people need less transience in their lives. They need to produce something enduring."

"Human compassion can be enduring. What did you say your profession was?"

"I'm an architect," I said.

"That's not exactly what you told Mack."

"All right. I design parking structures. Portable elevated parking structures."

"That's a permanent contribution to life?" she asked. My ears burned and I found myself focusing on her beadwork vest. In LA, people always told me they were grateful for what I did. "Nomads are a bit primitive, you know," I said.

Now she laughed. "That's what they've been saying since the beginning of civilization. The Romans defined nomads legally as animals. But cities are violent at a rate twenty times that of nomadic life. The violence goes back to Cain and Abel. Cain was the settler, remember. The Resident. Abel was the shepherd, the Nomad."

Could she be right? I asked myself. Cain the first land developer? Cain the architect of the first parking lot? Now I wanted to make her ears burn. "You people still use fossil fuels," I countered, even though I knew by now that the diesels were only used during storms. "Anyway, you're exaggerating the hostility."

She looked at me with measured skepticism. "What *about* Kill a Nomad Day? September first this year, right?"

"That's just sort of a drive-by thing," I said uneasily. "It could have happened to me, before Mack picked me up. I'll grant you this," I admitted, remembering the relief with which I left the shoulder of the freeway for even the strange rig. "Nomads have more compassion."

I took a deep breath. "At least I can still get out of your way. Mack said we'd make Hubbard's Cave tomorrow. I'll be gone. Back to my job, my neurotic fiancée, a Rotweiler who pees on my tires. I'm sorry we couldn't get along."

She looked at me. Something else irritated her now. "I'm sorry too," she said, and looked away.

◇

The sunrise was blinding red, all toxic haze. The complex swirl of looping wide ramps we were descending from the west culminated in a phantasmagoria of cloverleafs and delicate concrete columns supporting roads on a dozen levels. Traffic glinted in the sun, stretching east and south as far as I could see. A huge billboard under the signature of Mayor Richard Daley XXIII welcomed travelers to the Kennedy-TriState Interface at Chicago, "the largest intersection in the world."

There was something festive about the place, the carnival lettering of the sign, the red and blue flags of the moving Nomad markets. The legendary break in the membrane, Hubbard's Cave, turned out to be a wide tunnel where an expressway passed beneath Hubbard Street, so deep into the city it would take us all day to drive there. Mack described for me a set of service doors in the tunnel wall I'd be looking for, and I practiced stepping out of the cab as far down as the footplate.

The dry run turned into a close call. A gust pulled Ryder's cap from his head and he nearly tumbled off the rig snatching it. I grabbed a handful of his jacket and held on until he steadied himself, a dicey piece of footwork, it turned out, for me too. Acura gave me a grateful smile, then said she was embarrassed that she'd been so unfriendly the day before. So it looked like we'd be parting on good terms after all.

We made a turn southeast through the Jefferson Park district in late morning. The traffic of Chicago lay beside us, undulating like a sea. At Edens Junction, Ryder and I watched lane surfers jumping the median fence to run their ATV's back upstream, then downstream again at high speed, in elegant cuts across eight or ten lanes of waves of vehicles, touching bumpers as they slid by.

I was exhilarated and frightened by turns that day. We sighted the tunnel entrance first at four, an ugly wide maw in the distance swallowing traffic like Charybdis swallowing the sea. Ryder had been chattering away about how excited I must be going back to HoloGolf and BumperBusses in LA, but even he fell silent when we drove through the dim green lights surrounding the tunnel mouth and into the dark heart of it. It was a wild place, all roar and the whine of gears. The high-pitched scream of roller bearings wailed against some deep thumping in the guts of it all, like a slow evil heartbeat. Dust in the air intensified the darkness.

"It's up there," Mack said, squinting through the windshield at a faint glow ahead. "In that strip of yellow light on the right." We all squinted, trying to make sense of dark shapes moving ominously in dirty air. Mack interrupted my distracted goodbyes. "Something's wrong. I can't..."

We all saw the problem at once: down the ramp of a merging tunnel on our right rolled a fleet of four-by-fours, black pickups and vans with enormous soft tires. Sounding airhorns, they were surging forward, bumping the traffic ahead, rising over it, gyrating, crushing their way forward in purple light.

They were replicas of the truck I'd seen in LA, the one with the hood with the wolfish snout that had risen above the gridlock. The whole of the wide tunnel began to fill with the glistening black shapes as the fleet swept across the lanes on Nomads' roofs. The coppery tang of fear in my mouth turned bitter now.

Yet some part of me marveled at what I saw: What traffic! What a nightmare!

"How are you going to get out?" Ryder cried.

Two lanes over a Nomad work crew was crushed before our eyes as one of the monster trucks descended on a canvas-topped Omar. One of the four-by-fours took on a big articulated loadcarrier just ahead; a figure leaped down from the passenger's side of the truck with a chain saw.

"They're hijackers," Mack shouted.

Mack was driving for his life. A four-by-four started bouncing on us. Mack fended it off with a thick aluminum pole with a shotgun shell at its end, a bang stick, which he extended out of his window and fired against one of the monster truck's fat tires. The truck tumbled away into accumulating wreckage.

"The right lane's blocked," Ryder cried.

Through the twisted metal I could see peds fighting around the service doors in the membrane. I thought I saw one make it through. "Just get me close," I said.

"No," Acura said. "Don't go. It's too dangerous."

"A promise is a promise," I told her. "I can't ask for more from you good people. Goodbye."

A yellow van crashed on the left and burst into flame. I thought of just falling to the pavement and accepting my fate, but I resolved anew not to die in traffic without a fight. I took a deep breath and opened the door. Noise and bad air flooded the cabin. We were bumped again, from above, as I swung out. A monster truck's fat tire, near enough for me to feel its black heat on my face, bulged and quivered; in the din I heard a chainsaw start up.

Mack and Ryder and Acura were goners if the chainsaw cut through their roof. I saw an opening to the right but yelled for Mack's bang stick instead. I swung it up and blew the truck's tire, taking a scrape as the entire black shape slid between me and what had been my path to the service doors. They were already behind us. I thought about running back on the roofs of the slower vehicles and timed a leap for a wrecked trash hauler dead in its lane just as a diesel tanker rammed the wall and burst into flame.

"No," three voices screamed in the din. And as I jumped someone grabbed me, someone sweet-smelling and strong enough to pull me back through the door with a grunt.

"We'll try New York," Mack said as I slumped against the dash. "There's a place, the Core… You'll have a better shot. This is crazy…"

"… even if we have to drive back to LA," Acura said.

Ryder shouted that he saw the end of the tunnel, a white ring of daylight in the distance.

I was shivering with cold and fear. I felt Acura slipping something over my shoulders—the burgundy leather jacket Mack had let me wear days before.

The strange thing was how, when we were leaving the tunnel, another Nomad survivor waved in companionship, waved with the four raised fingers of the Nomad salute, waved directly at me. It felt pretty good to wave back.

We looped through Detroit. Mack had arranged for repairs and alterations to his rig, and we docked with an enormous moving custom shop.

We hadn't realized until Indiana how badly his left arm had been crushed fending off the first four-by-four. Acura became exhausted pulling extra shifts driving. Circling the freeways of Detroit in the gray air before we docked, I started driving shifts too. The rig seemed alive to me then, a huge powerful animal beneath my hands, a wounded animal, but one that would stay the course.

While they worked on the damage, I took in a number of Nomad Campfires—in Detroit, they burned scrap lumber—and listened to stories of pirates and Road Runners and feuds and radical rigs, threads in the fabric of Nomad lore. An old transmission specialist recreated tales of historic traffic jams so convincingly I forgot where I was.

"I dunno," Mack grumbled, a swath of bandages around his shoulder, his spirits low. "How the hell can you forget you're living on a conveyor belt?"

"But sometimes it's wonderful," I insisted. "Being a Nomad is like being one of those birds who are only really alive when they're in motion, like a tern, or an albatross. There's a poetic side."

"Now you're getting it," Acura said. And then she kissed me, a soft kiss on the cheek.

"I might even miss you when you're gone," she said.

Ryder rolled his eyes.

◇

We drove through Ontario, an idyll of flat land and small caravans. We crossed the Niagara into thick freight moving through Buffalo and made the turn downstate when we hit the Hudson River.

Four days out of Detroit, New York City traffic appeared in the distance as a tight Byzantine mosaic simmering under the late afternoon sun. The Nomad Way went underground, merged with the Interface they called The Core, then ascended into steep-walled canyons of glass and steel buildings whose only exits seemed gridlocked streets leading to gridlocked Avenues whose vestigial traffic signals served as standards for the electronic membrane, like buoys marking channels. The Nomads kept in motion somehow, backing and turning, creeping click by click downtown toward The Core's center with glacial inexorability.

Day turned to siren-filled night turned to bleak daylight once again. Residents on cross-streets and in storefronts watched us with indifference, watched the Nomad rigs streaked with road dirt from around the country as if they were all just loads of freight shifting through the lowest form of transport. Yet down the side streets we could see traffic that had been frozen in place for days, Residents making camp on the spot like Nomads, trucks, even buses, that had been abandoned, festive street markets, packs of derelicts around fires in drums, even silver-suited Residents fighting over cabs that were not likely to move until nightfall.

Although we knew they'd be coming, we all went pale when we saw the black pickups, the monster trucks, again on the third day. A fleet even bigger than the one that had swept through Hubbard's Cave rose on a cross-street and poured through a break in the electronic membrane so huge it seemed the four-bys had official sanction to harass and hijack Nomads.

This time drivers like Mack were ready. He hit a switch and his own newly installed, hyperextendable tires began to inflate and the rig began to rise and shift into sixteen-wheel drive. Using a pile of street rubble as a ramp we surged up over the back of a transfer cab onto the roofs of ordinary traffic, joining a second level bright in the sunlight between high-rises, our weight so broadly distributed we rode over the mass of Nomad rigs without crushing them. Then the big rigs like Mack's proceeded to scatter the lighter pickups of the hijackers and smear a few into the membrane. Even through the noise of chainsaws and gunshots and the gnashing of gears you could hear the Nomad cheers. We headed south toward Washington Square, our eventual destination, right down the famous Interface at Fifth Avenue, the new fleet of upper-level Nomad vehicles turning back two more attacks by swarms of black trucks.

I thought I was heading home to Denise that day. I played a last game of license plate poker with Ryder, sketched a shelf design to reorganize Acura's closet (parking lot architects do have some transferable skills), and tried to come to terms with my regrets. I volunteered for a last shift at the wheel so my friends would be rested when they turned to exit the Core.

So I was the first one to spot the trouble. We'd been prepared for the second level of traffic on lower Fifth (indeed, we were part of it); we'd been prepared for the gridlock in Washington Square. We'd even been prepared for the sight of the mangled bodies of those who didn't quite make it to the service door in the base of the Arch which led to a subway station and escape from Nomad territory.

But none of us were prepared for the sight and sound of a third generation of black trucks which rose above the second tier of traffic. These were huge sixty-four wheelers, big as houses, powered by gas turbines so loud their roar shook the city for blocks. They came from the lower east side, their enormous tires proceeding to crush even the bigger Nomad rigs on the second level beneath their treads. Heading toward the Arch was like accepting a fate as filling in a traffic sandwich, rigs above, rigs below.

"This traffic is awesome," Mack said. "It'll kill us. Maybe the only way to get you across is back in LA"

I realized then how good it felt to know I was going to keep riding with Mack and Acura and Ryder.

We bailed out of the west side of Washington Square. In New Jersey we picked up a load of freight to tow in order to pay our way, and settled back in for a non-stop to Los Angeles.

◇

We drove south through Kentucky, the days idyllic with Nomad music and warming weather. Near Lexington, I finished remodeling Ryder's bunk area, fixed the plumbing, and even worked on the auxiliary diesel, replacing glow-plugs. Acura asked if I thought about staying on the road.

It was not my best moment. I was trying to get pipe sealant from beneath my fingernails and the smell of grease out of my hair. "I miss my sensurround couch," I told her. "I miss my VR suit, I miss Denise—well, I dunno about Denise..." My stomach grumbled. "I miss Instant Lunch. I even miss making goddamned Instant Lunch in my cubicle at work."

"It really better than Mom's vegetable soup?" Ryder asked after a moment.

I closed my eyes, and remembered. "Okay, definitely not. And your mom's twice the woman Denise is."

"I can understand missing your dog," Ryder said.

"I didn't say I missed Rot. Truth is, he doesn't have enough space to be normal. He lives in Denise's parking space and pees on my tires. Denise could keep him."

"I noticed your hair's growing longer," Mack pitched in.

"You look good in Nomad clothes too, you know," Acura said.

"But who…? I mean whose rig? Who's willing to…?"

"We are," she said. "Me and Ryder and Mack."

◇

The first time I made love with Acura, among the pillows and quilts on the wide bed at the back of the rig, was during a deep moonless night. Afterwards, I cranked open the big hatch above us and we lay on our backs watching the sky together, her body warm against mine and sweet with the odors of spice and wild vanilla. The sky seemed huge, the stars brilliant. It felt like flying.

And that's how I came to stay.

Acura put it best. Traveling, she says, is good for the brain. It's true: you get a sense of physical and mental well-being from a journey. The monotony of settlement weaves patterns in the brain that make you feel tired and small; traveling makes you feel bigger.

"It's a spiritual thing," Acura says.

True again, I say. Every day's an act of renewal on the road. Why do you think they had pilgrimages in the old days? Dante's journey may have started in hell, but it got him to heaven.

Of course, had we really tried to get me back across in LA (I thought of dropping in to settle my affairs), I'm not sure I could have left The Way if I'd wanted to. All the in-city Interfaces had been blocked off when we returned—apparently from total gridlock in the urban corridor from Malibu south to San Diego. We had to transfer our load in Bakersfield.

On Mack's more pessimistic days, when his sore shoulder bothers him, he sees the increase in both city and Nomad traffic and the fleets of black trucks as indicative of a "swarming stage" in the cycle of human population. Some guy named Malthus wrote about it long ago. It's like the suicidal march of the lemmings in Scandinavia; the increased aggressive migrations signal an end for the species in global starvation.

But my new bunkmate is more positive. Each day is a new beginning, Acura says. The journey is eternal, each click a step along The Way, Il-Rah, The Tao. That's why, she says, we will find the human future in space, and why the first great travelers there will come from the ranks of the Nomads. Ryder's electronic school has already acquainted him with mobile launching.

The problems seem distant to me now, since we've crossed the land bridge from Alaska into Asia. Of course Nomads have been on the roads here for years—the first mobile factories came out of Thailand, the first great wheeled musk herds out of Ulaanbaatar.

Still, it's the experience of a lifetime to hit Outer Mongolia and watch the traffic finally start to thin out. The road is gold across the steppes in the morning light as we steer toward Irkutsk and thousands of clicks to drive.

NAME THAT MOON!

The lunar lander descended onto the dusty pad, the fading blue crescent on its side—the Blue Moon Resort's logo—lost in the rising dust. As the lander touched the pad, it yawed unsteadily before bumping gently back down.

Please, I prayed, *no glitches.* I looked at my watch: the media conference was scheduled to begin in two hours.

Finally, the lunar dust, the regolith, settled in low-grav slo-mo and the small Menelaus Crater that defined the equatorial end of the Sea of Serenity reemerged behind the pad, bright with sunlight, crisp with detail. That was my personal signal that I could safely proceed. I licked my lips and pushed the unfamiliar joystick to propel the transfer vehicle Stewart had assigned me for the event, a kind of pressurized minivan, into a docking with the lander. By docking, we bring our guests to the resort without the hassle of an EVA.

The treads of the transfer vehicle crunched satisfyingly over the regolith and onto the pad. When the docking collars started to engage at a meter's distance, I checked my softscreen one last time. To my dismay, Karl Pope, the Chief Editor of *Condé Nast Space Travel,* the man I'd come to pick up, was now listed as "scrubbed." I hurriedly called up the new data.

They'd sent his assistant, a woman named Claire Albricht.

Netsearch flashed a list of projects she'd been involved in—for Linux/Hilton, for The Aston Mazda Group. She was apparently a marketing whiz, but it was Karl Pope himself, one of the travel media's heavy hitters, we'd been counting on to give credibility to our press conference.

His loss was another blow. If our new marketing campaign couldn't raise our occupancy rate, Blue Moon would have to close. I pictured myself being fitted for one of those yellow helmets they wore at the mining camp, breathing dusty air, shoveling ore to be fired for Helium 3.

I peered out across the landscape through the big van window and took a deep breath. Above the rocky plain that formed the Sea of Serenity, Earth hung in the black sky like a milk-swirled pearl, immense and bright. Yet it was the sight of *Mare Serenitatis* itself, its vast rolling face cupped by bright far cliffs, that brought me peace, that settled and centered me.

Then a wild mass of strawberry blonde hair pushed through the docking membrane. She was in her mid-thirties, a bit shaky. My heart skipped a beat. Claire Albricht's bleary green eyes had a wounded quality, and her expression was unhappy, but none of that, not even her baggy radiation suit or her black lipstick, could hide the fact that she was an attractive woman.

"Welcome to Hyatt Regency Fiat Blue Moon," I said, helping her stow her spacecase. "I'm Charley Shackleton. Hyatt PR. Call me Shack."

"*Ugh,* Claire Albricht," she grunted, grabbing the armrest with one pale hand, bracing the other against the headliner.

"You're not going to float away," I reassured her. "There's gravity here."

"That was worse than flying to Australia."

"You'll feel better," I said. "Give it a day."

She glared out the big side window as I started up the transfer vehicle. "Where's the resort?" Claire Albricht asked.

She could keep the lipstick—too New York—but I liked her silver earrings, her long neck. "Ninety percent of the resort's below the surface," I explained, telling her something most guests know before they get here. "Protects everybody from impacts and temperature extremes—nights here get down to 240 below."

She closed her eyes. "What do you mean, impacts?"

I wondered if she'd even glanced at her information

packet. "Without an atmosphere to burn it up," I said, "space debris comes right in." I waved ahead at the pocked surface, the craters and scattered pits. "Which gives us our, um, moonscape."

"There's nothing here but rocks," she said flatly. "Nothing at all."

I bit my tongue. As we rounded the foot of the Menelaus Crater, the near folded cliffs of the Montes Haemus Range rose to form the equatorial border of the Sea. With Earth high behind us now, the shadowed curtains of rock were crowned by a sky brilliant with stars, all the colors of the rainbow shot through with white. "How about that?" I asked.

She frowned at the cliffs and blinked. "This has got to be the most desolate place I've ever seen."

"Well, there's lots to do," I said, feeling my jaw go tight. "Ice skating, swimming, golf. Three restaurants, a spa. We've got everything an Earthside resort's got."

The big dome sheltering our lobby swung into view, marked with the Blue Moon crescent. We passed a couple in pressurized suits riding a treaded golf cart toward the course inside the crater, a sign of life which only seemed to call attention to the twenty empty carts at the starter's pod. It was hard to hide our problem.

"I've been trying to imagine what would make it worthwhile for Hyatt to fly us all up. I mean, in these days of virtuality, a *press* conference?"

I docked at the canopied port without comment and let the valets take over. Truth to tell, it was United's extra-orbital division that was eating the expense of flying up the media. The new promotion was a last-ditch effort to keep business going for them, too.

Once inside, as the desk clerk took a retinal scan for room entry, I noticed how red-rimmed her eyes were, how watery. Wads of Kleenex stuck out of her pockets. As much as she annoyed me, I felt a wave of pity and restrained my impulse to book her next to the rattling icy machine in the Kepler Wing.

At least she noticed the Waterfall of Diana in the lobby, the one you walk behind on the way to the Atrium. "You'd never guess this was even possible," she said above its soft thunder as we passed into the big atrium. "And there's so much light."

There was vegetation too, and I directed her to a meandering path among leggy ferns and palms. "All thanks to our fusion plant up at the pole—we've got a great supply of Helium 3."

She extracted a wad of Kleenex the size of a baseball from a pocket and buried her nose in it. "This is such an awful day for me," she sniffled. I stood there, waiting for her to say something else, but she just kept blowing her nose, and so I took her by the elbow and led her toward her room, telling her about our flock of pigeons.

At the brass-doored elevators down, I looked over and she was glaring at me suspiciously. Head case, I decided. "Media presentation at two," I said brightly. "I'll bet you can't wait to get online and tell the world when you hear what this is about."

◇

Barry Stewart—Blue Moon Resort's General Manager—adjusted his blazer and glowered nervously, sweat beading just below his hairline. We had refitted our unused Copernicus Ballroom as a media center, complete with VR cameras for Earthside realtime holocast, full wall screens on three sides, net guides and browser pages windowed in. A full-screen hi-D/3D moonmap hovered behind the dais, the resort keyed in with bright colors. The techs had done a wonderful job.

The media reps we'd shuttled up were augmented by an equal number of our own employees to flesh out the crowd. Still, it was a disappointing sight: interns instead of editors (from *Orbit/Extrageo*), location scouts instead of producers (from *The Virtual Travel Channel*), small crews instead of live feeds (from *Extreme Outside and Space*), our fitness instructor instead of anybody (from *Offworld*). At the side door, I was trying to keep Stewart from taking another hit from the silver flask he'd started carrying.

"Barry," I said, "We're going to change history. Tell them that."

"This better goddamned work," he muttered.

Claire Albricht walked unsteadily into the room, creases in her jumpsuit, wild strands rising from her blonde hair. I sat her beside a giggling couple whom I introduced as prizewinners from *Osakahoneymoon* and she bared her teeth.

As usual, when the crunch came, Stewart was great. He paced back and forth on the little stage, first warming up the audience with stories from the Apollo landings, a holographic full moon radiant behind him. He told us of the resort's conception and heyday, how in the ten years it had been in operation we employees had developed a special relationship with "this dear old rock." Over the past few years, he explained, like a kindly uncle relating how a family had drifted apart, the residents of Earth seemed to forget about the moon and the amazingly engineered resort and spa through which it can be experienced. "Nowadays the traffic goes to the orbiting hotels, right? Sheraton Geosync, Caesar's Sky Palace, Satellite 6? Well, I'm here to tell you it's time to think *moon* again."

He took a deep breath and said, "I've had a vision…"

According to Stewart—and this was the first time I'd heard *this* version of the story—he'd been out on an extended EVA surveying the Apollo 11 site for a potential hotel excursion. Out there alone, he'd found himself thinking about the moon not just as a compelling landscape but as a presence, a spirit, though a spirit that lacked a face, some way to evoke it. He'd wanted to speak to it, he said, but there was no name to call it by.

It was a testament to his charm that a hush fell over the sixty cynical media people in that room.

"… leading me to the reason we've brought you here today. In cooperation with United Space, Hyatt Regency Fiat

Blue Moon is proud to announce a marketing campaign that will change the way humans will see the heavens—the way lovers and sailors and astronauts and astronomers will see the night sky—until the end of time."

Now he really had everyone's attention.

"Out there at Apollo site, I realized that, unlike every other body in the solar system—unlike every planet, unlike *their* moons, Titan, Phobos and Io, say—or even unlike asteroids Chiron, Hermes and Neseus. *Earth's moon*—now listen carefully—*Earth's moon does not have a name.*"

"Let me repeat: *the only completely natural satellite of Earth has no proper, formal name.*" He let the information sink in—it was one of those obvious arrangements that went unnoticed. "All through history, we haven't been using a 'name,' we've been using a 'term,' a *generic term,* 'moon' "—Stewart made the word sound cow-like, repulsive—"to signify a very unique place."

"It's time to correct this oversight. With the full compliance and authority of the International Astronomical Union, the official naming body for asteroids, comets, and stars, Hyatt Regency Fiat has secured rights in perpetuity to a proper name for Earth's moon." Stewart smiled. "I see from the data prompters that our audience is building Earthside," he observed.

The girl from *The Space Channel,* a chubby brunette with a battered headset, was scurrying around to check her live feed; all around the Copernicus Room equipment was being touched and tweaked.

"Of course, the *choice* of a name for the moon belongs to the human race as a whole. And so—listen carefully again—we've created a contest with a few simple rules. From the moment I initialize our dedicated netsite, NAME THAT MOON, we will take nominations and votes for a name for the moon. Individuals logging onto the site will be entitled to one vote per Earth day. The voting will continue around the clock for seven days. At the end of the week, the moon will have a new, official name."

Contest regs scrolled behind him as Stewart raised his right arm. "Please join us, citizens of Earth, as we NAME THAT MOON!"

When his arm came down the new Netsite washed over all the screens and the crowd in the Copernicus Room flitted around like carp at feeding time. Correspondents shouted questions, bumped one another, waved their arms to be recognized, shouldered their way to the center aisle. The *Osaka* couple stood on their chairs. It must have been too much for Claire Albricht, who I saw with her head in her hands.

Candace Yuen, from our marketing department, joined Stewart, describing how random voters would be chosen to win trips, mylar excursion suits, even have their names assigned to darkside craters. Above the din she started touting VR tours of the resort for the Earthside audience.

On the wallscreen behind the dais a list of names started to grow: Artemis, Hoku, Luna, New America... In the tally window, numbers were already starting to rise like the bounce from the audience. An excited crowd in low grav is distinctive: gestures are more expansive, heads bob, people move more. Stewart was taking questions, Candace was laughing, and I zeroed in on the tall Chinese editor from *Hyperwire*, who'd promised a week-long feature in real-time holo in exchange for the golf pass I had in my pocket.

I saw Claire Albricht again on my way out. She was alone against the back wall, looking dazed, her wad of Kleenex in her fist. Her lipstick was faded.

"What do you think?" I asked, sitting beside her, trying to be friendly.

She looked at me sideways. "This is a really bizarre idea. Who does Hyatt Fiat think it is? All the names here are so ancient. Greek. Roman."

"As a matter of *fact*," I informed her, "farside names are modern—craters named Oppenheimer and Fermi, the Sea of Moscow."

"Well, it's still pretty amazing." She shook her head. "When's my flight back?"

"What?"

"I'm ready to leave. When's my flight back?"

I exhaled through my teeth. "The deal with *Condé Nast* is, you're *supposed* to be putting together a story based on live reports. A *week's* worth. You're up here for the duration. Didn't you even know *that*?"

A dark look crossed her face. The largest wad of Kleenex I'd ever seen came out of her pocket and floated to her eyes like one of the plump misty cumulus that condense up in the dome.

This time my sympathy ran out. "You don't know the first thing about us," I told her. "You don't know why you're here. You're with us three hours and you already want to leave. Couldn't *Condé Nast* have spared someone who was at least remotely interested?"

The damp wad floated down and her eyes welled with tears. I heard a small voice.

"What?"

"I'm sorry," she said.

She buried her head in her hands and sobbed. Then she composed herself and looked at me bleary-eyed. "I s … said, I'm *sorry*. I'm sorry I'm taking it out on you. I've been having such an awful time. I broke up with … Oh, you don't know him. He and I, Karl and I…"

"Karl?"

"Three days ago, we're at Kennedy. He's booked to come here, I'm booked to go to Maui. I told him—and it's really hard to tell somebody it's over, you're supposed to do it in a public place, right? And he didn't get it. I mean, *I* broke up with him, gave him my rehearsed speech, and he doesn't understand. It gets so bad, I go, 'Don't you get it? You're *dumped*. What part of *I'm moving out of the condo* don't you get?' and the *next* thing I know…"

"Karl Pope? From *Condé Nast*?"

She sniffed, nodded. "I shouldn't have used the word

'dumped,' right? The next thing I know he takes *my* ticket to Maui and he gives me *his* to *here* and he goes, 'Goodbye, you bimbo.' He called me a *bimbo.* I knew I never should have dated my boss." She was burbling. "I feel so awful."

I sighed. "Well, Claire, listen. How about keeping us out of your plans for revenge. We're just trying to survive here. Maybe you've noticed?"

She sniffled. "That's a fact. You hardly have any real guests. Sorry."

"And you're not even a travel writer."

"Well, I *do* know about marketing," she said. "That's what I'm saying. You could be doing better."

"Is that right? Tell me about it."

"Would you be a little less pissed?"

"I could try."

She took a breath, blinked to clear her eyes. "OK. To begin with, you don't use your hotel manager to announce a campaign. That's so minor league. If you want real publicity, you get a celebrity. You get somebody who brings an audience with them."

"Like who?"

"Like, I don't know. Shirley Taylor. Lance Jason. Art Ball. Art Ball would have been perfect."

"Art Ball?" I snorted. "The talk show host? The one who's part Artificial Intelligence?" I pretended disbelief, but the truth was I listened to Art Ball myself. I'd even brought his name up with Candace, but after the look she'd given me, I'd been too embarrassed to take the idea further. "Art Ball's over a hundred and sixty years old. The human parts of him, anyway."

"He's got the largest single listening audience on Earth. Tops two billion." She sniffled. "Oh, *Earth.* I miss Earth."

"There's nothing I can do to fly you back," I said. "But look, you could have a good time while you're here if you'd give it a chance. We've got a pool, bars, a gym. Golf."

"My therapist did tell me to start something new, to get some exercise."

"There's a schedule downloaded to your softscreen. Banquet tonight. Moon range chicken."

She sniffled into the Kleenex. "I don't think I feel like eating."

"How about tomorrow? I'll show you some of our facilities." I checked my softscreen; I was booked for lunch with two Italian PR men. "I'll be free at two?"

"Ough," she said, sniffling. "Ough-kay."

◇

That night at midnight I sat on my bunk picking stringy chicken from my teeth, feeling sorry for myself—since Samantha'd left a year ago, my quarters just seemed empty. I was listening to web radio from Earthside, watching my autodialer strobe on my softscreen. To my surprise the faint flashing stopped, the speakerphone booted up, and a nasal voice said "Hello?" A hot flash of self-consciousness shot through my body. I cleared my throat.

"Uh, hello. Art?"

"Yes."

"Art Ball?"

"Well, who'd you expect?" the familiar voice of Art Ball groused over the speakerphone. "We don't have screeners here, like some other shows."

"First-time caller, long-time listener," I recited. "I can't believe I got through. Great show, Art."

"I'm getting a delay. Are you up on one of the satellites? At L1?"

"Calling from the moon, Art. This is Shack..."

"WELL, TURN YOUR RADIO DOWN, SHACK," Art Ball started bellowing. "BETTER YET, TURN IT *OFF*. HOW MANY TIMES DO I HAVE TO TELL YOU LISTENERS TO TURN YOUR RADIOS OFF WHEN YOU GET IN?"

I fumbled with my keypad to cut the speaker, my hand shaking. "Art? Still there?"

"That's better. What's on your mind?"

"Art, I know you're interested in the great adventure of space…"

"And what's your point?"

"I'm just saying, have you heard about that webvote, NAME THAT MOON?"

"Right."

"Art, it would be great to see the good people who are behind this incredible idea get a real show of interest…"

"Caller, are you one of our Helium 3 miners?"

"Uh, no."

A long silence filled my quarters. "Let me guess," Ball's voice snaked out like a slo-mo whip. "You're an employee of Hyatt Fiat. You know how we feel about the New Solar Order down here?"

"The *what*?" I vaguely recalled an old UN proposal that claimed sovereignty over the moon, to which Hyatt had signed off. Some glitch in Ball's AI software must have locked onto the Hyatt reference and his opposition to it. "Art," I said emphatically, "This is not a political thing…"

"You people think you can use my airtime for propaganda? Listen to this, Shack."

The signal went dead with a thunk. My face flushed, and my eyes burned. My speakerphone hissed with the vastness of space.

I gave Claire Albricht the tour, starting with the ice rink. We saw spectacular jumps and the rapture of average skaters working out their first triple axels in one-sixth gravity. A couple from Minnesota took turns launching 360 overflights at center ice.

After a night's sleep Claire looked refreshed, looked better than she deserved to look. Her lipstick today was dark plum, an improvement. She told me she wasn't much of an athlete.

"It's different here," I told her. "Low gravity."

My point was demonstrated when, on the way to showing her our diving boards—diving is like flying here—

we cut through a workout room with thick pads on its floor and filled with gymnastics equipment—parallel bars, rings, a pommel horse.

She grimaced. "Here's my torture chamber from high school."

"Try something."

"Aw…"

"Just one thing."

She took one low grav step toward a pommel horse without much enthusiasm. And, astonished, she found herself sitting on the horse. "Hey," she said, "that was … amazing."

She bounced down and tried it again.

Next she tried the parallel bars—slipped off, didn't hurt herself, bounced back up again. She was smiling like a kid. "I could never do anything like this on Earth."

We looked over the spa, the whirlpool, the climbing wall, the weight room, but we came back to the gymnastics equipment.

"Can I use this gym?"

"Right now, if you want to. The concierge will give you a locker, bring you the right clothes."

"Thanks," she said. "You're pretty nice after all. Can I get a rain check on your invitation?"

I thought of the Hubble Room, pricey even with the employee discount—though if the hotel was going to close in a week, it might be my last chance to eat there. "Lunch tomorrow," I said, and she said, "It's a date."

Later I checked in with Barry Stewart at the Copernicus Room. He was alone, though a quartet of remote VR cameras servoed back and forth from stations along the side walls and made it seem like we were being watched. That turned out to be wishful thinking.

"How'd our first day turn out?" I asked. Out of superstition, actually dread, I'd avoided looking at the website.

"Could be better," he mumbled. He was chewing his thumb.

I finally looked. "A hundred and sixty thousand votes total from Earthside?"

His expression was pained. "Actual hits less than projections," he said. "That number's a bit inflated."

I'd gotten close enough to where he sat hunched over a terminal to smell alcohol on his breath. He was wearing the same blazer he'd worn the previous night at the banquet—you could tell from the faux Bernaise sauce on his lapel. "It'll pick up," I said to cheer him. "Anyway, who's ahead?" I read from the wallscreen. "Diana. In second place, there's Artemis. All the old space junkies liked that name back in the last century, still do, I guess. I don't find an entry listed in third place."

"I'm, uh, leaving it off the official results. You know how we assign each voter a password to make sure they vote only once a day? Apparently the line about 'enter password' is confusing."

"Oh, Christ," I said. "You mean third place is 'password'?"

He worked on his thumb. "A quarter of the votes."

"Cripes. The moon could be named 'Password.' " I looked over his shoulder and saw a long list of what I took to be Native American names following "password" on his softscreen. "Some nice ideas," I said.

"Thanks," he said wryly. "I made those up."

A knot of Helium 3 miners crowded the stainless steel bar Claire and I passed through on our way to the Hubble Room the next day. Even dressed in clean red jumpsuits, the miners, men and women both, looked grubby, skinny from long-time low grav work, squinty-eyed from living in low light.

I steered Claire past. After a day working out in the spa and pool she looked vibrant and healthy, looked great, which didn't escape one of the male miners, who clowned falling off his barstool.

"I still don't get it," Claire was saying. "What's wrong with the word 'moon'?"

"It's not a *name*," I told her, pulling her chair back. The Hubble Room overlooked the southern end of the pool, just above the waterfall up in the atrium, just below the level at which clouds formed late in the lunar cycle. It was our grandest spot. "The word 'moon' comes from an Old Germanic base for the word 'month,' which itself comes from the IndoEuropean word for measure. A 'moon' is a device to measure time in the sky. It's not a proper name."

"Luna, then. The ancient name is Luna." She waved vaguely at our false sky, the inside of the dome, painted with fanciful stars and our blue crescent logo.

"A second-rank Roman goddess. I looked her up. Not a single legend to her credit. And the name's never stuck. You say to somebody in Manhattan, let's go to Luna, they think you mean some town in upstate New York."

"Artemis?"

"Another name that sounds like a town upstate, but otherwise an excellent candidate. Artemis was Apollo's sister. Moon, sun. Still second in the voting."

"According to my sources, your contract with the Astronomical Union's airtight, so I guess it's going to be your call." She scanned her menu. "Heavenly Fettucini and Moon Pie. Cute."

I noticed her nose was still a bit red.

"And what are you going to do if the hotel closes?" she asked.

"It's hard for me to imagine leaving," I told her.

She rolled her eyes. "Believe it or not, I'm just having salad. I'm signed up for back-to-back aerobics classes."

Claire skipped the evening's banquet. I drank too much at the United party afterwards and wound up stopping at the Copernicus Room around midnight. Candace was there with a triple Cappuccino. Stewart's tie was askew, his voice hollow.

I could smell something different on his breath—he'd switched to Southern Comfort, a bad sign."Look at this..." he muttered. "How can the Lakota sue us over the name Hatara? We can't be 'appropriating' that name. I made it up."

"They made it up first," Candace pointed out.

I looked at the other traffic. "What's this 'Moonbeam Laser' product?" I asked. "Can *they* really sue us?"

"Check out the message from 'Wicken.org,' " Candace said. "When the lawyers have some free time, they should look into the legality of this curse."

"It's awful," Stewart said. "Even bookings are down. What did we do wrong?"

I shrugged, staring dully at the holo moon on the front wall, cycling through its phases.

"Shack?"

"The only plausible explanation I've heard so far is that we need a celebrity spokesman."

"Like who?" he snorted. "Art Ball?"

"Well," I said as brightly as I could, "I think I heard somebody mention his name."

Candace laughed so hard she shot Cappuccino out her nose.

◇

Claire Albricht had turned into a low-grav exercise junkie. She put in hours on the "big steps," in aerobics classes, and on the gymnastics equipment, swam for countless laps, even started diving from the ten-meter board. I stopped by to watch her—by her invitation—as I took breaks from full buffet breakfasts, media briefings, cocktail parties, ten-course banquets.

She was fun to watch. Moonies are skinny. She had some flesh.

On day four she invited *me* to lunch at the juice bar next to the spa.

"I hope I'm not being a pest," I said. "Everybody else is lizarding out in the Jacuzzis, pigging out in the banquets."

"I used to do that," she said. "Now I feel like a new person. Karl is so history. As if I hadn't already made it on my own."

"Ah."

"It's true. I was Director of Marketing for The Four Seasons. Which has to do with my plan for when I get back." The new Claire had stopped wearing lipstick altogether. She still had a little red around her nose, but otherwise looked great, her skin smooth and fresh, her eyes clear and bright.

My eyes, on the other hand, felt like they had sand in them. "Wish I had your drive," I said, "your resilience."

"You need a plan, too, for when this place folds. When I get back to New York I'm going to set up a consulting firm in resort marketing. You're a sharp guy. That kind of job would work for you. Relocate and I'll hire you."

"Like I say, I can't imagine living anywhere else."

"What do you see in bare rocks?"

"You haven't gone outside yet, have you?"

"Hands full right here, thanks. Get in shape before I go back, be ready for it." She actually rubbed her hands together; she was wonderful, all energy and enthusiasm; you could see the rosin embedded in her palms. She smiled at me. "Though I could take a break."

My heart skipped a beat. "There's a trip I have to take tomorrow," I told her. "A long ride out in the transfer van to the Armstrong Site. How about coming along?"

◇

That night, late, I lay on my bunk listening to Web audio again, that great throwback. Of course we run on a different "day" up here, with our light/dark cycle adjusted to Earth's, so my atrium window was a soft blanket of darkness.

"Thanks for taking my call, Art," I heard a male voice say, a voice heavy with a tired slur, a familiar voice. The hair rose on the back of my neck and I sat up. "First-time caller, long-time listener, Art," the voice said.

I heard the clink of a silver flask. I could almost smell the thick sweetness of Southern Comfort.

The call was brief, even by Art Ball standards. "We have a voiceprint on you, General Manager Stewart," Art Ball snarled. "We're not taking calls from you New Solar Order people."

You could hear Barry starting to protest as he was cut off, but only half his word came out, and his "Arrrr..." made him sound like a dog.

"Wildcard line, east of the Urals, you're on the air," Art said to someone else. "Can you imagine that guy?"

◇

"A road?" Claire said. "A road on the moon?"

"A track," I corrected her. "Nobody's allowed to build a road on the moon. This isn't something you can see from Earth. We run semi-inflated treads and make a hundred kilometers per hour without leaving much impact—the embedded track guides us around boulders, crevasses, collapsed lava tubes."

She moved the picnic basket the hotel kitchen had packed for us back with the folding chairs and tables, the crates of bunting, the box of collector-quality flags, the EVA suits, the spare life-support stuff, the tools. My assignment was to scout a media event at Tranquility Base—Stewart was considering pulling out all the stops—and the rear of the transfer van was stuffed with equipment we'd want down there.

Claire leaned against the thick Lexan window, trying to get a better view. "It's so different when you're not spacesick," she mused. "So clear. It's like my eyesight's better."

"No atmosphere," I reminded her.

In my mirror Blue Moon's main dome was receding rapidly. Ahead lay boulders and craters sprinkled across the regolith stretching away to the horizon, a horizon on which you could see the very shape of the moon's curvature.

"Amazing," Claire agreed.

I accelerated and toggled in the object radar to avoid any unpleasant surprises.

"This is really out there," she said quietly.

◇

The run to the '69 landing site, Tranquility Base, takes you east along Plinius Crater. From there what we now called Armstrong Site is a straight drive south across the center of the other major lowland in this quadrant of the moon, the *Mare Tranquillitatis*. To reach the site, you traverse the Sea of Tranquility until you reach a long feature called the Rima Hypotia, just north of the lunar equator, and then you turn east.

Along the way, especially near Plinius, you encounter ridging, massive rimes and collapsed lava tubes, but those aside, you also see wonderful flat patches across the regolith. You see every kind of landscape the moon offers.

We had a long talk, Claire and I, as we drove. I recalled how as a kid my dad had told me about watching the first moon landing when *he* was a kid and how, when I'd first set foot on the original landing site, I'd felt connected to him in a way that had surprised me, connected with some dream of his in that Detroit suburb in whose backyard he watched the heavens. Maybe I was overdoing it, but even now, I told Claire, Tranquility Base seemed to me a sacred spot, a spiritual place, not unlike Machu Picchu, I suggested. "Or Haleakala, that enormous high caldera in Hawaii."

"That's where I've seen this landscape before," she mused. "It's like being around the Hawaii volcanoes."

"Only up here it goes on forever. That's what I like about the lunar surface," I told her. "It's raw planet, as primitive as it gets."

"You don't want to see it become terraformed?"

"Not me. I like it just the way it is. Full of promise. Old and tough and full of promise."

She saw it first, a reflected blip of light from the replica lunar lander that had been installed at the site. "There it is," she said.

Sure enough, in the middle distance the spidery legs and

drum-shaped body glinted in the sunlight. We closed in quickly.

"There's the American flag," Claire said when she spotted the little Old Glory left by Armstrong, with its horizontal batten to make it wave. I started telling her how it had been knocked flat when the Apollo crew had taken off, and how NASA had reconstructed the site, when she wondered out loud about debris around the lander. I thought at first she was seeing the scientific instruments the crew had left behind, the ESAP equipment, the passive seismometer.

Then I noticed the crude writing on the lander's side.

The childish yellow letters read, NOTHING COULD BE FINER THAN TO MAKE IT WITH A MINER.

I brought the van to a stop, rubbed my eyes, and sighed. "I don't suppose I should be surprised," I said. "They tagged the starter's pod on the golf course last year with the same color paint."

Ration wrappers and beer tubes littered the site near a burst waste cylinder. The white bunting hanging from the ladder turned out to be toilet paper. "They've trashed the whole site." To my great dismay I saw dozens of fresh bootprints stomped at the foot of the lander's ladder.

"So rude," Claire said. "Those people from the bar?"

"Two years ago they put laundry soap in the Falls of Diana."

"So adolescent. That tag is obscene."

I unbuckled my harness and moved some cartons to fish out the toolbox and service supplies. After rooting around I turned up with a can of hydraulic fluid in the emergency kit. Then I started struggling into my EVA suit.

"Where are you going?"

"I think this'll get the paint off," I told her, waving the can. "I'm going to try to restore things as best I can and clean up out there. But hey," I added when I saw her pulling on the baggy leggings, "not you."

"I wouldn't miss this for the world."

◇

Once on the surface, Claire bounced around in her silver EVA suit like a kid at soccer practice. "Look at Earth," she blurted when she caught her breath. "So bright and blue and white. Walking around out here, it's like heaven, like I'm in heaven."

As for me, I felt like hell until I saw how well the hydraulic fluid dissolved the yellow paint from the metal shell of the replica lunar lander. I used the bunting I'd brought along to rub it clean. It took a while. Eventually I improvised a rake out of the LEM ladder and started to systematically wipe miner footprints from the regolith near the lander. Claire walked ahead, picking up litter, stowing it, detrashing the site.

As I raked, I realized that Armstrong's famous bootprint was in there somewhere, but I had no choice except to obliterate it along with the miners'. When Claire finished her sweep of the site, she came around behind me and scattered handfuls of regolith to obscure the little furrows from my rake. It sounds easy enough, but out there in the clumsy suits, it was slow going.

Two and a half hours later, Tranquility Base looked like a museum exhibit again, except for the missing Armstrong footprint.

As it was perhaps the most famous single footprint in human history, we needed to replace it somehow. First we downloaded archival images from NASA's website and studied them carefully. My plan was to step gingerly *on* the passive seismometer so as not to leave tracks, then to bounce up the ladder and position myself as Armstrong had. From there it would be a simple matter of a hard step down from the bottom rung.

"Wait," Claire said.

"Make it quick," I said. "We've got about twenty minutes before we get into reserve life support."

"What's your boot size?"

"Eleven 2E. Does it matter?"

"According to NASA archives, Armstrong had small feet. His boot size was nine and a half. *Narrow*."

"Where the hell are we going to find such small feet?"

She pointed down to her boots. "Nine and half. Narrow."

So we traded places. "One small step for Claire," she said just before she jumped. "One large step for all Clairekind."

◇

We'd lost so much time cleaning up the site, I radioed in a negative report on the scouting trip and we had to drive straight back. Still, the drive was breathtaking, the sun high and slow across the sky, the Earth slipping to our left and then setting. We were both a little giddy at what we'd done.

From the moment we docked at the main dome, you could sense that the atmosphere at the resort had turned hectic. Less than twenty-four hours remained until the contest's conclusion. More Hyatt people had come up to join the partygoing journalists and hotel guests in a kind of last day's frenzy of food and wine and excess.

The big table on the dais in the Copernicus Room was askew, crowded with half-empty glasses of wine, coffee cups and abandoned room service plates littered with stale food. I found Stewart stretched across three chairs in the corner, drunk and sullen. Candace, who had been conducting virtual press conferences Earthside since early morning, was desperate, her voice hoarse. I took over for her, worked for eight hours straight, fielding questions and calls, infusing false cheer into our dismal numbers, pretending surprise and pride that "Luna," ahead all week, looked like it was going to finish first.

Claire and I became separated once I started to work, but then she really disappeared, into the gym, I supposed, or to take a nap after our excursion. Then it was dinnertime and I'd been too busy to connect with her, and I frankly was relieved that she wasn't there for the humiliation of the final night's banquet—half the chairs empty, Stewart incoherent and helped to his room. During the gazpacho I was passed a note from Claire telling me she'd gone out on another EVA, entirely on her own, a walk around the dome to collect some rocks to take home, that she would find me later.

But when I looked for her at midnight, she was nowhere to be found. I dragged myself off to my room, fatigued beyond belief after the long day, and threw myself on my bunk.

◇

I couldn't sleep. An active solar flare sent a wave of broadband static across all the communications channels, and the web audio link I lay there listening to reminded me of radio in the old days, fading in and out, conversations washed by flurries of audio snow…

"Loyal caller, long-time listener, Art," a female voice said, a voice velvet with seductive breathiness, a siren's voice, eerily familiar. "Call me 'Heavenly Ten.' I used to call you from Earth. Remember me? You were so my hero."

Art's voice changed. "My god, I *do* remember you. Is that you, 'California Ten'? It's been … years. What can I do for you?"

Art recognized it too, or at least the program of his AI did, some deeply enduring quality of that voice. I remembered hearing a voice like that while listening to Art Ball when I was a kid. Almost all of Art's callers, then as now, were men, but once in a while you'd hear that siren's voice and the whole conversation changed, moved as if a step to the side. The voice seemed to speak directly to an old subroutine in the AI, to open a secret trapdoor: Ball had always had a weak spot for women who did call, not for the tough ones or the airheads, but especially for women whose breathy voices promised some unseen sybaritic redemption—as his audience had been mostly male, the old-fashioned attitudes had been part of his appeal. The trapdoor was apparently still programmed in the AI, and you could hear him responding.

"I'm *so* mad at you, Art," the voice pouted.

"Oh my god, *why*?" And you could hear it, the genuine nervousness in his voice, the uncertain edge that comes from loss of confidence.

"You betrayed all of us women who love you when you blew off that moon contest. If you'd only supported it, think how many of us would be looking up there right now. And next week and the week after that. Gazing at the moon because it meant something." I thought, *Candace*? Then remembered her hoarse voice. Still, something familiar. "But that's all right," the voice went on. "I understand, Art, why a romantic idea like NAME THAT MOON wouldn't appeal to you. You're too old to be romantic anymore. I'll bet you never sit with Ramona outside your trailer in Parump looking at the moon on a beautiful night…"

"Awwwoh," Art moaned. "You know, Ten? You might be right. It would have been romantic."

"Might be?"

"Ramona is going to be annoyed with me."

"As she ought to be. You're letting those liberals from the New Solar Order pick the name of the moon."

Art moaned again. "What name do you suggest? Just tell me. I'll log onto that website and vote myself."

"What really matters is that your listeners call." Now I heard something else in the voice, a kind of marketing savvy hiding behind the voice-changing circuit.

A couple more sentences and I was sure. The voice belonged to Claire.

I looked at the time. Two a.m., twelve hours until the end of the contest. It was too late now to change the result, I decided. Still, I was touched down to my toes and smiled as I shut down all the circuits in my cubicle and settled back on my pillow. I told myself: Claire had tried to help, and it would all be over soon.

I overslept. When I woke I took a long, hot shower, and slowly got dressed without logging in. On the final day of the contest, at the final hour, I went directly to the Copernicus Room to see the wreckage.

Barry Stewart, I was surprised to see, was on his feet, wearing a fresh suit and clean shaven. He was gesturing with animation to a larger knot of media people than I'd seen all week. Judging from equipment logos, new techs had also flown up. I recognized four network heavy hitters in the restricted area behind the dais, covering the story in holo presence. There was a special electricity in the room. A middle-aged guy with a recent face-lift waved cheerfully to me from another crowd, I waved back—he looked very familiar, but I couldn't recall his name. Candace came striding by and I asked her who he was.

"That's Karl Pope, you dummy," she said in her hoarse voice, stopping, looking me in the eye, cocking her head. "Didn't you hear he'd flown up from Maui?" She smiled. "Though you of all people, I shouldn't be calling dummy. I apologize."

"For…?"

She rolled her eyes and shook her head, turning away from me with her arms raised, leaving me to stare at the wallscreen. The full moon cycled in the repeated time-lapse pattern that had been pixeled in all week, overlaid with our numbers. I blinked, rubbed my eyes in disbelief.

Overnight we'd gone from eighty million hits on our netsite to three and a half billion Earthside voters.

And that's how the moon came to be named Art Ball.

It is a strange result, I agree, as loony as Art Ball himself, and six months later, as I write this story, the moon's new official name is still too improbable for most people to take seriously. But the attention the new name created nonetheless saved us. Our bookings immediately shot up six hundred percent and the reservations site clogged with traffic. As you probably know, we're booked solid to the end of the decade and we're planning to excavate a new wing. What with all the extra flights United's put on, the United/Hyatt consortium's already started work on another landing pad.

Yet for all its odd quality, you do hear the moon called Art Ball up here once in a while (particularly among the miners), and you certainly do hear the name used more and more Earthside. Good-natured people look to the night sky and turn to one another with smiles and say, "Art Ball." All over the world, I'm told, kids have started pointing up and telling their friends that you can see his eyes, his face. Claire and I sat through a movie just last night, a remake of Huck Finn set on a Mars mission, and midway back to Earth the Huck character turned to the Jim character and said, looking to Earth's moon, "There he is. There's Art Ball."

When you live on the moon for a while, you adjust to its rhythms. After we celebrated the end of the contest, after Claire explained how she'd used voiceprints from Art Ball's archives to identify the AI's weak spot, and after she got her chance to spurn Karl Pope one more time, most of the media people flew back to Earth. Claire stayed on and we watched Earth set earlier and earlier in the shadowy coming of the real end of a lunar day.

On our way back from Tranquility Base, Claire had promised to spend a night with me, and I talked her into a trip for the two of us over an entire lunar darkcycle, fourteen days. Barry got me the keys to the spacehab module at Aitken Basin, near the moon's south pole. We both took leaves and I drove the van down there.

At twenty-two hundred kilometers in diameter, the Aitken Basin is one of the largest craters in the solar system. It's a grand sight, all right, but that's not why we went down there.

Inside the basin is a smaller crater, large enough by Earth standards, but tucked inside the basin with a group of two others. This crater is the Shackleton Crater (yes, named after my great great grandfather, Ernest, of Antarctic fame). The spacehab module we drove to is parked at the point where the west rim of the Shackleton crater intersects with the rims of the two other craters, forming a peak twelve hundred meters above the basin floor and canted at just the right angle to escape Earth's shadow. Because the sun falls on this patch of ground day and night virtually year-round, the Dutch astronomer Ockels called this spot "the peak of eternal light." Solar panels placed on the peak generate continuous power to the module, keeping it warm and cozy, the love nest of preference in Earth's orbit. EVA walks are spectacular. It's as if you had the Grand Canyon, Haleakala Caldera, and Everest, absolutely all to yourself.

After a couple of days, Claire found herself pointing out how small a dot New York made when you looked for it, squinted hard, tried to make out its lights at night. "Just a dot," I remember her saying that day, curled on a sheepskin by the big Lexan window. "From here New York is so just a dot. I can't tell you how much I've gotten to like it here. This is the ultimate place to get away from it all."

The day we'd left Blue Moon I'd turned down an unsolicited job offer, the best that had turned up so far, to be the head of PR for the Moorea Beach Hotel. When I could turn my back on the best Tahiti had to offer, I knew my heart belonged on the moon. That Claire wanted to stay here as well meant my heart would be full.

She handled some of the rocks she'd picked up earlier in the day, rocks for a collection she'd started the day we'd gone to Tranquility Base. She'd noticed that not all the moon rocks were of a uniform charcoal cast. Seen up close, many had subtle hints of color in them, trace elements and their oxides, the building blocks of Earth, hints of ocher and umber and copper and gold, silver and white, deep reds and darker browns—all the colors of life hidden in the raw rock.

"Like Barry said," I told her. "There's a job for you up here if you want it. A life."

"Count me in," she said, snuggling close.

I buried my face in her soft hair.

A half hour later, as we sat looking at the milk-swirled blue pearl in the sky, she asked, "What do you think Barry'll want me to do?"

"Marketing," I shrugged. "Work with Candace."

She was looking at Earth through the big window. "Mmmm, Shack?" Claire finally said. "You know, I'm just thinking, well, for later? Like I say, I'm just thinking, and maybe you know?"

"Know what, Claire?"

"Technically speaking, is 'Earth' a proper name?"

REPUBLIC

You know of course why we left, and what crews like ours were looking for. I said, *why we left*. I meant, of course, *why we had to leave*. Those years before *The Copernicus* began its passage seem like a dream to me now, the home world a green idyll, the night sky all white moon, the sunrise off the sea on the day we launched oranges and reds, a wild mango sky. Northward, the mosquito coast shimmered silver in the rising sun.

I'm sorry. I'm already running on. I'm old now, three times old if you count cryosleep. There's so much on my mind.

What I'm trying to say is, that day from docking orbit you could see the lower atmosphere smoldering with the first city fires. All though our training years we'd seen the slow, sad, entropic fall of things, rubble where there'd been buildings, a rabble and drum fires on streets where there'd been traffic and order. Less than a year after docking, we left the home system. We never saw what happened, never saw those images you've now shown us on the screen. They'll take some time to absorb.

I'll tell our story as concisely as I can. Captain Hess is dead. I don't know how much time we have to talk—we never expected to be in communication again, never really expected to make it back. I'm the linguist who was sent with the mission. You have to hear about what we've seen. There is another world.

◇

Arcturus Wormhole—56 on the Mauna Kea grid—spun us

out in a region so dense with electromagnetic noise that we worried for our instruments. Our primary assignment was to plot the transit of the wormhole across a navigable sun, so we buried ourselves in the work until it was done. Only then did we really look around.

I've ported over all the recon data. You can judge for yourself. You can gauge the planetary masses, the orbits, the size of the star. The system is so like ours that we thought that, after sixty years of travel, we had arrived where we had begun. Our mission scientists were all either nav team or extraction geologists, like Captain Hess. After two days, *Copernicus* SciCom decided the objects were mirror worlds, sets of shadow planets, something like that. Hess shrugged and dropped the question. An extraction geologist doesn't care where the minerals come from.

The fourth planet classified as tropical/marine. Its atmosphere? See the data stream, the lower atomic weights? You can imagine our excitement, our exhilaration, when that gas spectrometry came in. It's one of the things we—the first generation crews—were sent out to find. Tropical/marine with breathable atmosphere was the great good place, the golden fleece *The Copernicus* was looking for. Then X-ray spectrometry described parallel chemical and biological processes with Earth.

Yes, *biological*. Now look at the EXO screen.

An intelligent race.

◇

Geophysics had sent ahead an unmanned orbiter to collect data, and when we saw that EXO screen, we realized that a series of rectilinear surface features was a chain of settlements. Two hundred clicks apart, each maybe ten clicks across. Nav was happy, we'd gotten good data on the transit, now planetary geophysics was ringing all its bells. Before we knew it, close probes produced the miracle of a language we could deal with. It was so much more than we'd expected.

I have to tell you right off that it was too much for our

EXO to deal with, too much for the whole default EXO program to deal with. The original EXO had a stroke and died in cryo, so they gave the job to Lieutenant Grace, the backup shuttle pilot. Like I say, all the rest of our scientists were nav or geo; they would have had even less idea what to do.

Anyway, from orbit we could see that the settlements were socially complex but technologically primitive. Wheels, metals, sanitation, all of it on first glance pre-electrical, and first glance had most of it right, except for some process through which they charged their weapons. But they're not savages. They have art, abstract processes.

And that language. From the first, the hard vowels, those inflections… I told myself that since the phonemes were produced by similar cranial structures, the language had to sound that way. But there was the echo of something else, something structural. Have you ever heard of Linear B?

They are very much like us, more like us in some ways than ourselves, Grace liked to say. Not that you would mistake them for human, as you can see from the screen. Thin as rails, articulated trunks. But that fabric that group is swaddled in? All that geometrical body ornamentation?

Initially nav put *The Copernicus* in a parking orbit and we deliberated. Imagine rebreathing your own gasses for sixty years, the three hundred of us squeezed together, recycling fluids, solid wastes. The whole crew was fixated on the oxygen spike in the atmosphere. Adamowski, our Flight Surgeon, could see what was coming. Eventually, he wanted protocols the rest of us couldn't deliver. When Hess organized the first shuttle down, he had already locked himself in quarantine.

By then the marines were on high alert. I didn't like the run-up, the predation vids they immersed themselves in. I remember Sergeant Vrask hunched in her cubicle, submerged in the glow of a bloody hologame, her breath short and damp. It's true there was a lot of warlike activity on the surface. It's true that within an hour of landing we saw spilled blood. Rust red, if you please. But they are civilized beings. I'm sure of it. It's in the language.

◇

I was with the first down shuttle. We slid through pink cumulus towers so beautiful that some of us wept. We landed ten clicks from a settlement, on a grassy plain away from dwellings—the far end of a farm, it turned out.

Perhaps they'd seen us in low orbit. At any rate, we were greeted—they touched their hands to their heads, and bowed, and kept back, then knelt, and touched their hands to their heads and bowed. That's when we saw those geometric patterns for the first time, in their body art, in their fabrics, in their personal effects.

There we stood in our bulky white suits. Our EXO—Lieutenant Grace—was waving through a series of contact gestures programmed by some bloody semioticist back on Earth a century before. Nobody knew what he was doing, not even Grace. You could see him tracking the manual on his helmet monitor. We were all a bit giddy, even Vrask. Captain Hess started laughing. While that was going on, Mercer, the chief scientist, knelt beside an alien, and the two of them started sorting out words with gestures and whispers—ship, sky, rock, hand. You could see Grace's frustration. The Arcturus probes hadn't even hinted at life. Hess had never given him time to train.

◇

Eventually, a larger group marched up from the settlement, marched in order, its hierarchy transparent. The dozen aliens who had been with us—local farmers, it turned out—touched their foreheads to the soil and scattered. The chiefs among the newcomers were wrapped in red and silver capes, the capes so intricately folded they brought to mind origami. There was also a language in the folds, a hieratic sequence, the same sequence that was conjugated in the rank words they used, a series of inflected long vowels, shifting from a to e, so half the time you thought they were chanting. A slow moving elder whose cape was the most elaborate was the head of them all. The society was at least as hierarchical as ours—it was in the way they walked, in the way they stood, it was in their silver eyes. The language mirrored it all.

A group of ceremonial guards performed a whirling dance, slicing the air with those long rods, and then they pushed a deer-like animal into a circle. The rods functioned as weapons—they were javelins, swords, Kendo *shinai*, all in one. They slaughtered the animal. Our first sight of blood. It was a ritual act, so we tried not to draw conclusions. Still, I don't think we were prepared for the violence or for the sound of the animal's cry. As it died it sounded human.

Anyway, the rods. Their grips were so finely worked with that intricate geometry they seemed like jewelry, though what they were were personalized weapons. The aliens always had theirs at hand, used them in ceremonies, even charged them electrically in a way we never quite understood.

Hess kept his distance. The marines made the first real contact, even while they respected basic quarantine. I mean they were the first to make any sort of connection. After a day we sent the bulky EVA suits back up orbit and traded them for hermetic jumps and light breathing helmets. The aliens were always nearby, and the marines were obsessed with them from the first deer. The marines showed up each dusk when the ritual animal was released. They tracked its run, they tracked the aliens' every move in pursuit, focused on the white knives with the same rapture you saw reflected in their eyes in the hologames. In just a day a camaraderie developed between them and the hunters, and they gestured in admiration narrating how the deer was brought down. They compared weapons, handled the rods as best they could while keeping quarantine with the breathing helmets and jumps. You could see them awkwardly stepping and swinging through the basic moves, as if they were learning a dance, a physical language.

After three days—*The Copernicus* in orbit, the lander and the cargo sled shuttling down to a base they'd laid out for us, quarantine holding—we were invited into the city. At midday we were led in a procession through narrow streets and stone buildings and across squat bridges over a series of canals and waterworks that ringed the city center. We finally reached an eight-sided plaza acres across at the river, at a fortified stone bank. A temple dominated the land side. We'd seen the river from orbit. It was so wide that from where we stood we couldn't see its opposite bank. The site had been developed with defense in mind: the temple was protected by the rainbow of canals at its back, and by the fortified stone bank along the river at its front.

We were so caught up in the alien architecture, the strange symbols, the high narrow doors, that most of us missed the obvious, missed what was happening with Hess, what *had been* happening with Hess. From the first the aliens had been deferential to him in the extreme; I wondered if I was misreading language from an unfamiliar body. But that afternoon, when we entered the city, the children ran ahead and paved the street with broad leaves for Hess to walk on. Several thousand aliens came out of their dwellings and chanted as he passed. They kept their distance and bowed, touched their foreheads to the soil.

The reality only became clear to me as I watched them bestow a cape on Hess's shoulders in the eight-sided plaza. They wouldn't look directly into his eyes. The cape was blue and gold, but it otherwise matched the folds of a cape on a statue to one side of the temple door.

They had decided that Hess was something like a god.

The tall alien we had seen earlier made a speech from the foot of the central stairs of the temple, which the crew asked me to translate, so I made my guesses and said welcome, god from the sky. Hess still didn't quite get it. He asked me, *How much longer*? I told him he had to respond, and he just looked at me, annoyed and confused. It was an awkward moment.

That's when Grace stepped forward, reached around behind his neck and pulled off his breathing helmet.

So he was the one who broke our promise to Adamowski. Grace waved his arms in a wide circle, raised them to the sky and took a deep breath. The rest of us were transfixed at the breaking of quarantine.

Before anybody could stop him Grace stepped out of his jumps and started chanting a greeting he'd composed. You could tell he'd poured himself into it, thought it out as best he could, and rehearsed. He had their vocal range, for what it was worth, and his hand movements were a semiotic catalogue of compliance and interest. He knew Hess didn't quite get what was going on. Grace was trying to negotiate contact.

At what turned into the end of his performance, he touched the tall alien in the yellow and red cape, just touched him. Understand that that same alien had put his hands on Grace before he'd pulled his helmet off. He'd touched his suit, his faceplate, his gloved hand.

But when Grace touched him, the ceremonial guard surged forward. Grace was challenged with a weapon, one of those rods, but this one crackled with energy. Grace fell back with a burn on his shoulder.

The tall alien apparently was something like a god, too.

Grace pushed himself up, bent with pain. In slow motion, head lowered, hands open, he moved through a vocabulary of conciliatory body language. I thought he might be killed until Hess stepped forward. Hess had this flat, firm voice, and he gave a long speech about misunderstanding protocol as if he was lecturing to lab assistants. His confidence was a wonder—he still didn't know what was going on but to the aliens, anyway, he acted like a god. That's why we survived. We were all of us anxious from the bloody show we'd been seeing with the deer. That day it seemed like every hour you could hear one cry.

In the meantime, Vrask had moved to one side and slipped out of her helmet too, to protect Grace, I guess. You could hear her breathing hard. When she peeled off her jumps she was strapped with weapons, and the weapons distracted the ceremonial guard while Hess was speaking. By then Vrask's troops were shedding helmets and suits, too. And then when

I looked, of all things, Vrask begins showing an alien her weapon, turning it in her hands, clearing its chamber, offering its stock to an alien elder. In a blink, the aliens visibly relaxed, and the marines were smiling, and they were comparing weapons with the aliens again, now the other way around. The tension dissolved between them, or maybe it was never there for the leaders to exploit. That's why I used the word "bonding."

Captain Hess read into the log that we "shook it off" once we were all of us out of our suits. The air smelled sharp and fresh, like cut grass—it was wonderful to take off that breathing helmet. But I didn't know what to think.

◇

The next day they presented me with the Codexes I've holocopied in the Appendix.

I've been working on them ever since. There are structural echoes of an ancient script, one of our protolanguages… I could be wrong. Remember that Linear B I mentioned? There were so many echoes it seemed to me hallucinatory, like living out a parable or a dream. How to account for it? Earlier contact? Coincidence?

Copernicus/SciCom was no help. When they could be dragged away from either nav data or mineral samples they only shrugged. It wasn't clear if the way Hess was treated rubbed off on the rest of us. I've never really been able to translate the language—there's another level of coding in it, I'm certain. There was a lot of confusion that week. I suppose there still is.

◇

Ten days after we had first touched down, the aliens declared a citywide holiday in our honor. Their voices naturally produced an overtone, so their singing was particularly alien, aggressive and sad at once. We sat with them, tried their words, handled their tools, played with their pets. They taught our marines an exercise with the rods, then challenged them to ritual sports. Aside from the rods, they threw copper like stars with sharpened points well enough to bring down a deer at thirty meters. Vrask and her people showed off their own skills, hand to hand stuff, target work with those compound crossbows they train with. The aliens loved the handheld hologames. They loved them. The remains of any shadow seemed to lift and we stopped thinking about the business with Grace. By then most of the crew got a turn downplanet, even the hydroponics team. In the end there was a dance. Those tubes are musical instruments, that moving line a dance. Can you see how it replicates the figure on the elder's cape? To tell you the truth, it felt wonderful to move in a natural gravity. Just being alive seemed a wonder.

I suppose SciCom had it right. The aliens thought of us as emissaries of one of their sky gods, his name all long vowels. The god, in person, they figured was Hess. Hess just grinned and took mineral samples. He ate the food. He was afraid of nothing. The only one who never broke quarantine was Adamowski. For all those weeks when the rest of us downplanet were feasting and basking in our kinship with a god, he was up there, locked in containment.

Grace was desperate to redeem himself. That's why he took them for trips in the cargo sled. That's why he showed them how the shuttle worked, how you could run anything, really, with just a keypad controller from the hologames and the right codes.

I'll try to stick to the main things, to what happened. It's just that certain details seem preternaturally clear now—the human cry of the deer, the aliens' four fingered hands, strong enough to crush a man's windpipe, their children's wooden toys, which seemed so human. Hess showed me a mineral once which changed color when he shattered it, exposed it to atmosphere, rainbow sand running through his fingers.

And I remember those pink clouds and the blue of the sky. Have you ever seen a robin's egg? When I looked up I squinted and I thought I saw heaven. But some nights I would look up and see only strange stars in alien constellations and I would feel lost beyond any recovering.

Have I told you what they did with the blood? About the ritual at the cave? To mark the end of their training, their ceremonial guards are taken, blindfolded, at night, to the scene of a fresh battle at the edge of their territory. That's how the planet's organized—one self-sufficient city against the next, shifting alliances, constant low level war on their perimeters. In torchlight, the initiates kneel, cup their hand against a fresh wound. Then they are told to bring their hands to their mouth and drink the blood.

Did I tell you our marines were invited along? That some of the marines drank the blood as well? Some of them had reactions, but the others... I think it kept them from being sick later. I believe they were being recruited. You know some of them stayed. The fresh battle to which they'd gone was a smoldering fire. The planet was already destabilizing, the news of our arrival spreading like the rosy light of the sun. And now we were part of it, the marines, their weapons, even Grace was part of it, with the business in the cave.

That's where he was killed, three days after the first blood ceremony.

◇

We were never really sure who killed Grace. Captain Hess withdrew all but a skeleton crew up to *The Copernicus*. We reviewed our data, took inventory of our samples—geologists, planetary engineers, people like me. It was possible that Grace could have been killed by one of our own. He'd been strangled. Hess decided that we should ship back home.

We held a service for Grace and a ritual farewell with the aliens, who gave us no answers about Grace. We were happy enough to leave.

We hit our mark to the wormhole, initiated cryo sequence, and out of nowhere, our primary engine fell apart on us. The core blew out our water, blew out a side of tanks. You know how little water we carry, how we just loop it around. Well, if you lose half your holding tanks, you have a problem.

We had to return to the surface of the fourth planet to resupply. We jury-rigged the cargo sled with a backup tank from hydroponics and used the lander for logistics.

◇

There was no welcoming committee this time. Even the farmers kept their distance.

We established a site beside a lake three clicks from our original base. There was trouble. First tools started to go missing, then materials, starting with pipe at the shoreline. Gloves, boots, then a rebreather. When Hess complained, one of the silver and red caped elders gave him a sharp lecture. I'd finally gotten familiar enough with the language to translate: we were taking something of theirs, their water. They had the right to take something in return.

I told you the planet was tropical/marine. It was awash. Still, in their language, the word for water was the word for life.

As the crew was squaring away the sled after topping off, the aliens decoupled the tank from the cargo sled's cab, the cab with the power unit, and three of them took the cab and lurched off across the lake.

Hess had been up orbit. He was livid. He dressed in his ceremonial blues and went down with the marines in full gear. The farmers led him up the shoreline on a false trail for three hours—it was a total waste of time, they'd convinced him to go on foot, it had turned hot, and he was tinder. He marched the squad through the stone buildings and into the square between the temple and the fortified bank, followed by a crowd. He made for the residence beside the temple.

His idea was to take an alien as hostage for the cargo sled's cab.

But the instant Captain Hess raised his arm to seize the elder, a guard ghosted up from behind and made a sharp, sideways move with his rod that made Hess' head snap forward. Weapons went off... It was a real mess.

We took on the rest of the water under fire. Seven marines deserted, hooked up with the aliens who had hijacked the cab. We had it in mind to forcibly extract them but we had to leave when we realized that weapons had been pilfered along with the cab and that they were being trained on *The Copernicus*.

◇

We set course for home.

Adamowski had been right all along. Downplanet crew started turning up sick immediately. Adamowski guessed disease was wiping out the aliens, too. Even before we left parking orbit, the great elder was dead, though with the sled's weapons and the deserted marines for a time his group must have ruled the planet.

We saw the evidence that the marines and weapons had been a tipping point on our way out of the system; in the year it took us, we could see a transformation in the pattern of settlements, a consolidation, then what might have been a collapse.

Most of the crew died in that year before reinsertion.

If our journey out seems a dream, our journey back, those years on *The Copernicus*, seem dark sleep itself, dreamless sleep, the black night of cryo and faint stars as we crawled through the wormhole.

Adamowski died tending to the sick. That's why there are only eighteen of us left, that's why there are so few survivors listed on the manifest.

◇

It was a pleasure to talk with you yesterday. You're breaking up today as well. Of course it's a shame to have come so close, only to be made so certain that we could never land. You will forgive my attack of nostalgia—*nostos*, from the Greek, for home; *algia*, also from the Greek, for pain. Pain for home. We understand that there's no choice but for you to apply a strict quarantine. We understand the potential for severe measures if we approach. You will appreciate the irony. We came back willing to make do with what might be left, and we were worried that it might not be safe to land. Now that Earth is restored, a garden where there had been a smoldering wasteland, Earth has become the very place we can never land. Once we thought we were the lucky ones.

When we signed on with *The Copernicus,* we thought the trip would be the adventure of our lives. Now we know the trip was our lives.

Is our lives.

That's why the eighteen of us are turning *The Copernicus* back.

We're reinstalled the original program. We still have plenty of reactor time to power the drive. We want to see those pink clouds again. We want to die off the ship. We're curious about what happened to Vrask and the six other marines. They didn't get sick, as maybe you've realized, because they're the ones who went through the alien initiation, they're the ones who drank the blood.

Have you also asked yourself why the eighteen of us survived? Why if all the other members of the crew died of disease, why we're still alive? I'm guessing that you have.

Yes, to be perfectly frank, yes, all eighteen of us drank the blood as well. I apologize for not telling you in the first place. We brought alien blood to our lips just after Grace had been killed. The communion transformed us. When we were forced to go back for the water, when the fighting started, when the rods began humming and they pulled the white knives from their sheathes, we could kill with an energy and indifference none of us had ever felt before. Maybe we're a little less human for that, but it kept us alive, you know, seemed like a vaccine against death itself. Maybe it means we belong to the place. And so we'll go back. There are still things hidden in the language to me and I'm curious to understand just what we've done.

BLUE FLYERS

The kangaroo, a young female, gazed at them from just beyond the electric fence which ran parallel to the tarmac at the entrance to the resort. She had liquid brown eyes with long lashes and dilated pupils. Bipedally erect, alert, she stared with inscrutable wariness at the two women who'd stopped their bright red electric skimmer on the shoulder. The older woman, who'd pulled back the skimmer's reflective cover, tried to meet the animal's untamed eye.

Valerie Rampling shivered. "Is she…?"

"No, she hasn't been implanted," her Latino driver smiled. "She's free range out here. In another year she'll be ready, I suspect." The driver—her pale plum safari shirt was adorned with the triangular BioRange symbol which crowned the entrance gate—waved a manicured hand over the scrubby Cabo San Lucas landscape toward the groups of three or four kangaroos scattered on a low hillside a click away. Some were larger animals with reddish fur and white faces. "She belongs to that mob over there—the word for a herd of kangaroos is 'mob,' yes? With those boomers. Males. In that species, the males are redder, the females bluer, you see?"

"You keep them with males?" The kangaroo she was watching at the silver wire spooked her. Above its outsized haunches its tiny, perfectly articulated forepaws picked slowly at a patch of chest fur, too slowly for grooming. The blue flyer had the face of a deer or a pony. But the twitchiness of her large ears and the intensity in her eyes made Valerie think: a monkey, she reminds me of a monkey, an intelligent monkey. Valerie took a deep breath of the overheated Baja air. Under the circumstances, she decided, she should be relieved, even pleased. But she hadn't expected to be surprised this way, especially since she'd been looking at so many pictures of kangaroos lately.

"Under BioRange protocol," the Latino driver said, "we don't use freerange flyers to carry an individual fetus to term." She laughed. "So nobody's baby's out there. The Carriers, the marsupials whose pouches have been genetically designed for use as surrogate human wombs, they're kept under quite controlled conditions."

"Yes. Of course." Valerie felt briefly ashamed: she knew all these things from the introductory holos she'd seen in New York. She remembered shots of the nurseries, buildings which were half-barn, half-hospital ward, where the implanted animals were kept in great security and health while within their pouches the human fetuses became full-sized, normal infants.

Her Ob-Gyn had agreed that having her baby this way was a particularly fine idea. Very practical. At twelve weeks her pregnancy hadn't, except for this flight down to Baja, interrupted her legal practice for a day. Tomorrow her fetus would be transferred to the marsupial's pouch where it would mature without another bout of morning sickness for her, much less the loss of a single billable hour for her firm.

Twenty minutes later the resort and clinic buildings came into view beyond a green patch of woods in a wide groin formed at the base of two hills, a change of scenery from the deserty scrub through which they'd driven from the airstrip. What she saw reassured her: an elegant Mission-style hotel, flanked on one side by pools and tennis courts, on the other by a hospital and labs. Nestled in groves against the hills sat the adobe nurseries with their red tile roofs.

Before the bellboy could reach the skimmer, a tall fellow with a cream-colored Stetson and deep-set eyes reached into the trunk for her bags. He had a BioRange triangle embroidered on the pocket of his denim shirt, an easy smile, and a low whistle for her short silk jumpdress when she stepped onto the tiled foyer.

"Saw you at the gate, ma'am. My name's Cal."

"I'm sure it is," she said, turning away without telling him her name, but smiling. She'd spent a summer in Wyoming once; there was something Disney City about this cowboy, though she couldn't put her finger on just what.

◇

Her pre-surgery screening was scheduled at four—the transplant would be performed the next day. Once she unpacked, Valerie decided to wash off the dust of Baja with a swim.

Flowering mimosa trees lined the walkway to the pool, opposite Spanish fountains which spilled cooled air into the burning heat. At poolside she dropped her wrap on a chair near a group of women chatting under a market umbrella, then dove in.

The water was in the low eighties, clean and sweet, the pool so large that when she swam under the waterfall at the far end she had to tread water for a minute to catch her breath. Everything seemed perfect now; even the anger of Kenneth, her child's father, at her decision, even his threats, washed from her mind. As she climbed out she heard one of the women calling her name.

It took Valerie a moment to place the blonde with the narrow hips. "I'll be damned. Kai. It's been ten years."

Kai Olsen had been a classmate at Dartmouth.

Kai introduced her with some pride. "And Val's the best advert lawyer on Wall Street. She's been on SELF."

"I just found myself more comfortable in front of a console than anywhere else," Valerie admitted, telling them the same thing she'd told the videozine.

Kai had been at BioRange for two months, it turned out, staying on through her pregnancy like the other three women, all of whom had suffered previous miscarriages. It was one of the options at BioRange Cabo. "And you?" Kai asked.

Val laughed tightly, feeling the rhythm of Manhattan still in her bones. "I'll be back at work by the end of the week."

The women around the table looked at her with polite interest, as if they were impressed. But their eyes were glazing over, and one resumed her knitting.

Val felt herself blush. Across the pool on the access road an old ATV had come to a stop, an odd-looking sort of truck without a windshield and crowned with a rack of spotlights. Kai and her friends smiled and watched. The cowboy stepped out, straining his jeans, and waved to them. Three of the women waved back, giggling flirtatiously.

Walking quickly back to her room Val asked herself: why should I feel ashamed?

◇

At her four o'clock appointment, her transplant specialist, a matronly female surgeon, completed her screening physical in under a half hour. In her cool office she shifted a flatscreen around to show Valerie a high-definition sonogram of the fetus in her womb. "Looks wonderful," Dr. Levich said. "We'll have a perfect match."

Val squinted. "So, um, the umbilical cord gets connected to the marsupial, um, pouch?" Now she wished she knew more.

"It's a bit more complicated. The macropodid pouch provides different kinds of teats for joeys at different stages of development. We use the one appropriate for a first phase joey, who's continuously attached for several months. Our flyers have been genetically designed to retain that teat indefinitely. The point is to make the pouch a suitable environment for poikilothermic young."

"Poikilo…?"

"Poikilothermic. A human fetus, like the first phase joey, is unable to control its body heat, so it needs a host who'll do so with her nutrient supply. Secondary to the teat, we attach the umbilical cord of your fetus to a tiny umbilicus the marsupial produces when her joey's embryonic. So we tap into the blood supply as well as the nutrient loop before we suture the pouch. Given bodyweight and chemistry, and one antibodies injection, we can duplicate the conditions of your womb perfectly.

Though we want just the right blue flyer, of course." Dr. Levich looked at her watch. "Would you like to see her? The Carrier we've selected for you?"

Valerie agreed and finished dressing. During the walk from the hospital building to the nurseries, she told Dr. Levich how Kenneth had objected to the procedure, how he'd filed a restraining order to keep her from leaving New York, how he'd threatened her. "He's a younger attorney in my firm. But we're not married, of course, so..."

"Only one in six children is born to married couples these days," Dr. Levich told her sympathetically. "And only one in four is delivered vaginally. What does he want, an abnormal child?"

Her blue flyer was lying in a clean stall on the ground floor. Val remarked on her broad, flat feet, like those of an oversized rabbit, her substantial haunches, her immaculate blue-grey fur, her narrow shoulders, her long neck. When the lab attendant opened the Dutch top-of-cage door for them, the animal lurched up and moved to the rear of the stall. She kept her eyes on Dr. Levich for a minute, then seemed to grow curious. Bent over, not quite on all fours, balancing with her tail, she shuffled closer and worked her lips.

"Notice the shaved patch at the pouch," Dr. Levich said, leaning over the gate and holding out a handful of meter-long grass. "She's been prepped for a week. That's our standard window to see if there are any complications." Dr. Levich bunched the grass and tossed it along the steel wall and the kangaroo stretched over to reach for it with her snout.

The way she worked the grass in her mouth reminded Valerie of a cow. In fact, there was something very docile, bovine, about this blue flyer. Like her Aunt Nell, Val decided with a smile—and the 'roo had her aunt's smoky blue hair. "How soon do you know after the surgery if everything's going to be OK?"

"We usually know within twenty-four hours, but technically the window is ten days. Of course we have back-up animals."

With a metallic clang that startled the three of them, a door on the outside wall of the stall opened. Hot air wafted through the nursery and from outside came a series of harsh, explosive coughs.

"Ach," Dr. Levich muttered. "Exercise time. We have a yard with a controlled mob. They're nocturnal animals, of course, so we send them out late in the day for an hour. Wonderful for circulation—in the wild kangaroos will carry a joey to fifteen pounds, easily."

The kangaroo had come bipedally alert and frozen. She was making a soft sucking sound. Valerie saw some feral quality in the marsupial's brown eyes now. She remembered the animal she had seen at the entrance gate: gentle as a deer but there'd been something hidden in her intelligent eyes. Val leaned over to see out of doors.

"Stay back," Dr. Levich warned. "A cornered kangaroo can lash up with its hindpaws. The males can disembowel an attacker at close range."

Val's stomach fluttered; she was afraid for her child in an irrational way she never expected of herself.

Back in her room she phoned the desk clerk, then punched up her office number in New York. She left a voice mail message to tell her partners that she was extending her leave for a week.

◇

Under general anesthesia, her surgery proceeded as if in a dream. But her sleep afterwards was disturbed by strange visions. She heard screaming, saw vivid colors. When Dr. Levich spoke to her post-op, the grey-haired physician suggested that she'd been mildly hallucinating—a side effect of the new delta-series anesthetics.

Her suture line was just an inch long. They'd gone in with a laparoscope, a small, flexible surgical instrument that had penetrated her abdominal wall. In a week, the nurse told her, she wouldn't feel a thing. In the meantime she felt a deep local pain, and when they transferred her back to her room, she felt woozy stepping from the wheelchair to her bed. She was glad she'd elected to stay.

◇

The next morning she was up and around, even polished off a room-service plate bright with papayas and huevos rancheros. True to form, the moment of the transplant Kenneth had filed a lawsuit for custody of the fetus, but a judge had already dismissed it. Her abdominal pain persisted but was bearable.

Over at the nursery she found that the blue flyer wasn't doing as well. The kangaroo—whom she'd come to think of as Nell, after her aunt—lay panting on her side in her stall, listless and indifferent to the fresh grass lying nearby. The suture line closing her pouch ran as wide as Val's outstretched hand; she'd obviously had a far more serious operation. Val was alarmed by the thick yellow fluid which oozed from the marsupial's pouch.

"Perfectly normal," Dr. Levich told her when she came in for rounds. With Nell so tractable, Dr. Levich brought Val into the stall during the examination.

"Her eyes look so ... vacant," Val murmured. A scorched, medicinal odor pervaded the room; it seemed an effort for the kangaroo to breathe, and her muscles were slack.

"Would you like to help with her care?" Dr. Levich asked. "Some mothers find doing so very reassuring. You see the recovery for yourself."

A veterinary nurse, a young man with a mustache, taught Val how to sponge off the animal's forearms to cool her, how to massage her neck. He showed her how to hold Nell still while he injected antibiotics. Nell's blue fur was as soft as down, her body hot, rising and falling with her breath.

For several days Val stayed close to the blue flyer, nursing her, grooming her, even cleaning smeared feces from her tail. She watched her regain her appetite, felt her muscle tone return. Once, as the kangaroo nibbled hormone supplements from the palm of her hand, she experienced an intimacy, she thought, with some intelligence behind the bovine brown eyes. Love my baby, she wanted to tell her; love my baby as your own. But a moment later the marsupial carrying her child nipped her thumb so hard she tore flesh, drew blood, and bruised her to the bone.

◇

Late the next day an ozone-sharp thunderstorm turned the exercise yard briefly into mud. Nell had been let out before Val arrived, and cleaning her was a wet, messy, tedious operation. The odor of the yellow fluid still oozing from her suture line was particularly noxious. When she kicked Val in the thigh, Val's instincts—even a slight disgust—told her it was time to back off from the nursing.

Still, she felt vindicated: her child's Carrier was feeding well and regaining vitality. That morning's HD sonogram had shown her fetus to be thriving, perfectly indifferent to the change of place. As Valerie Rampling locked the stall behind her, she realized that her own condition was better, too. Her head felt remarkably clear; her stomach muscles rippled painlessly under her hand. It was time to get on with life.

Just outside, the cowboy, Cal, was hosing down the muddy ramp from the exercise pen, managing to stay spotless in the process. The night before, at a torchlit dinner, Kai had alluded to his sexual prowess with lurid motions of her long-fingered hands, butter from a lobster sauce glistening on her silver nails. Now as Val passed, he smiled at her broadly, as if he'd shared the secret with her himself.

Her first impulse was to be offended, but the truth was she felt sexy for the first time in weeks. "So what goes on around here?" she asked.

"Offrange," he grinned, his jaws tight with the effort of shutting down the high-pressure hose. He pushed his Stetson back, looked up to the hills. In the aftermath of the thunderstorm the bruised red light over the hills was giving way to a clear evening sky, vast and sublime. "If you're interested, we can go for a cruise in the ATV, take a ride."

She took a deep breath. "I'm game," she decided, even though there was something wrong about the way he looked: his face was pale. All the cowboys she'd ever seen had dark tans that ended only at the precise lines at which they wore their Stetsons. His face wasn't tanned at all.

The walk to the motor pool took them through the clinic complex. As they passed behind the surgery Val heard a high-pitched scream that made her shiver. "Doesn't sound human," she said.

" 'S not." Cal told her that the flyers didn't take happily to implanting; beyond a certain point in the procedure, the use of anesthetics endangered the human fetus, and so... Even though her sympathy was checked by the throbbing in her thumb, Val felt her face flush. "Best not think of it," he advised, reading her mind. "This time of day, prob'ly just new animals settlin' in." With his soothing voice, with his deep set eyes, with the way his muscles moved beneath his clothes like some sensuous dream, she understood now what the other women saw in him.

The truck-like ATV was spartan, its suspension so stiff it made her teeth chatter, but it was refreshing to ride in a vehicle without restraining belts or a windshield. As the sun set with tropical swiftness they rattled overland through the hills. Fifteen minutes beyond the BioRange border they spotted a mob of wild kangaroos beginning their nightly rounds. "They got a territory," Cal told her, coming to a stop, "couple hundred square clicks. No electric fence from here to the gulf."

"Could they get away?" she wondered in the deep twilight. "I mean, if we tried to catch them with this ATV?"

"They make sixty, seventy clicks an hour, don't care what they get into—a 'roo can jump a ten-meter gully easy. But we don't have to chase 'em." Cal flipped a switch on the dash and with a high amperage thump the rack of lights above the cab burst into illumination, freezing the animals in their tracks like deer caught in a skimmer's headlights.

It took her breath away to see them standing like statues.

He pulled up close enough for her to see the light reflecting off the pupils of their eyes.

Cal pointed out the dominant male, a broad-chested red among a half-dozen blues.

His size and belligerent stance made her think immediately of Kenneth. And the 'roo's fur was long and shaggy, like Kenneth's hair.

Yesterday she'd learned that her console at the office had been trashed—Kenneth was her prime suspect. This morning the electronic mail had brought the news that he'd entered a writ in the Circuit Court of Manhattan to deny her maternity leave when the child was born. And her apartment had been broken into. All this while claiming he wanted to get back together with her.

Cal was still running on about the bull male kangaroo. "... almost seven feet. That boomer'll go 200 pounds."

There was something about the way he spoke, the way he was pointing his right arm through the windshield. Now she recognized the contours of the locked case behind their heads. "You hunt them, don't you," she said, half to herself.

Cal just stared straight ahead, chewing the inside of his cheek.

Dominant males, she sighed. The kangaroo, his sex hung between his massive haunches, barred his teeth. She could almost see Kenneth out there glaring back at them.

Cal, taking her silence for an argument, finally cleared his throat and muttered a few sentences about wildlife management.

She laughed. What would it be like, what would it be like, she wondered, to kill a boomer, to kill one of the bulls?

They drove into Cortez, a village whose inhabitants had been displaced some years before by the construction of BioRange. She discovered in its dirty cantina a side of Cabo she hadn't been prepared for: a cracked holoscreen, flies around the food, homemade tequila and a genetically mutated wallaby in a cage behind the bar, its double tail flecked iridescent green. The locals spoke a Spanish-English dialect she could barely understand, but Cal seemed at home.

Shabby customers drifted in and out. A man with a pockmarked face tried to sell them a laserblade which sputtered defectively as he tried to demonstrate its ability to cut through a thousand-peso coin. When he said he'd throw in a vial of drugs, Cal laughed him away.

"Had enough excitement?" Cal asked after her fourth tequila, stroking her forearm.

She hadn't, not by a long shot. She felt free now. She'd been released from her pregnancy by the transplant, extricated from the confines of the stall by Nell's recovery, liberated from her anxiety by the alcohol—and now, she decided, she was finished entirely, irrevocably, with Kenneth. Even when the pale cowboy told her "it might get rough," she wanted to stay.

Still she was shocked when only a few tequilas later, the cantina filled with tough-looking men. Two kangaroos in harnesses were dragged out from a back room, live kangaroos with harried eyes. They were herded into a makeshift ring that materialized between the bar and the tables. The adolescent boomers were goaded electronically—she watched the bartender operate a joystick, watched the kangaroos twitch under the harnesses—and set to boxing amid shouted bets.

"This is ... cruel," she said in the din.

"C'mon," Cal answered mildly. "They're only animals."

A dirty boy hopped around the perimeter of the ring making fun of the creatures. An old man with brown teeth badgered her and Cal for drinks, pointing to the boy, yelling, as far as she could make out, that there were wild boys out in the scrub hopping around in the moonlight like kangaroos, village legends the gringos never heard but which for the price of a bottle of tequila he could tell. By the end of the second fight she was too drunk to stand. She eventually found herself behind the cantina watching two kangaroos have sex. "Rough enough for you?" Cal asked, running his hands under her dress. In the uneven light the bull mounted the flyer brutally, filling the air with explosive coughs.

She pushed Cal away. She was disgusted by how aroused she'd become, by the gamy kangaroos, by the leering crowd who watched them. "No," she said. "Take me home. Take me home or I'll have you arrested for goddamned assault."

And then she passed out.

◇

The next day, her head ached and pain began to migrate through her midsection in slow searing waves, doubling her up with cramps so excruciating that she skipped a late breakfast to wait an hour in an outpatient lounge while the receptionist tried to fit her into Dr. Levich's schedule. Val sat feeling oily with shame, though in the moon-blue light of the ride back to Cabo, she'd recovered consciousness—Manhattan tough, after all. But the pain near her suture line alarmed her.

Dr. Levich diagnosed no medical problem beyond the severe gastrointestinal effects of a hangover about whose origins Val had to be purposely vague—the terms of her medical agreement with BioRange were technically voided beyond its borders. "If you celebrate with village tequila," the gray-haired woman said with a knowing smile, "you feel this way again. Yes?" As Dr. Levich rattled on about the benefits of transplants in avoiding fetal alcohol syndrome, Val half-listened, dressing with relief in an examining room whose walls were covered with anatomical charts.

One of the mauve charts caught her attention. A quick study of "The Macropodid Reproductive System" confirmed that the introductory holos didn't tell you everything. Each of the Carriers had to be pregnant already, pregnant with a joey, when the human fetus was introduced. The joey was terminated. According to fine mauve print, in that way the nutritional systems were in place and the hormonal levels appropriate to carrying young. "Is this right?" she asked the doctor. "When the human fetus is implanted, the joey is destroyed?"

"Mmmm. Yes."

"So my own blue flyer, last week?"

"Yes. It is not a problem. The mother still has a fetus, you see? There's no enzyme spike, no change in blood volume. So she misses nothing."

A kind of remorse led her back to the nursery. Today she found Nell lying on her side in the stall bloated with supplements, her suture line an angry red from being picked at. Val changed her straw, cleaned her water dish, and groomed her with a fine-toothed steel comb. She caught up with the changes in her chart and talked with the veterinary nurse about treating the swelling with a diuretic—already on his mind, he told her. With her help he injected the medication into the animal's forearm. Its onset was rapid: brighter eyes, less labored respiration. But within hours Nell turned hostile again, fouling the stall, baring her teeth beneath an inscrutable gaze. Val wished the nursing was as easy as law; she could handle cool screens and paperwork better than an animal's waste. At least, she told herself, she had the sense to leave Nell in the hands of BioRange personnel. Her own child was doing well; the word they used after the last sonogram was "thriving"; that was what mattered.

What she hadn't counted on was the power Kenneth still had over her. She'd thought she was immune.

His Holofax Tableau was delivered to her at poolside while she was sharing a goodbye margarita with Kai. Kenneth apparently now was into guerrilla theater. The Tableau, breathtakingly expensive to transmit even at off-peak rates, was time-stamped the night before. Val and Kai watched Kenneth perform in bed with a short brunette, a tart Val recognized from research. The scene shimmered obscenely from atmospheric signal noise generated by a high inversion layer over the desert.

She'd been naive enough to believe him when he'd said he still wanted to see her. Naked, he looked like a bull, like the boomer she'd seen on the hillside near Cortez.

The Latino driver who'd brought her in on the first day stopped her in the lobby, saw she'd been crying. "Don't let him get the better," the girl in the plum-colored shirt said after she'd sat Val down and they'd talked. "You have to be strong."

◇

"I didn't expect to see you again," Cal said when she located him in the motor pool.

"Tell me about the hunting," she said.

"Now don't get excited. We only cull the wild mobs, the surplus animals destroyin' the range. They overgraze like goats. That's why the ranchers wiped them clean out of Australia, if you wanna look into it."

"I'm leaving tomorrow. I want to ride with you tonight."

Cal gave her a wry smile and sucked his teeth.

"Don't be nervous. I just want to take one shot. If you let me ride with you, listen: I'll make it up to you in a way you'll never forget." She stepped close, placed her palm flat on his chest, slipped her fingers between two buttons. "That's a contract. You take me and I'll take you—on another ride."

Cal passed her a bottle of tequila when they set off.

She could see the inversion layer to the north, the bruised quality in the twilight sky against which helicopters hovered in the distance. At one point in the holofax Kenneth had looked straight into the 'corder, his eyes blank as shell casings, between rounds of frantic sex. "This is for you, Val," he'd said, pointing his index finger at the lens, pulling his third finger like the trigger of a pistol. "This is for you."

◇

Under infrared nightscope Val watched the kangaroos grazing in groups of three to five, munching vegetation like cows. Their oversize ears tracked the low rumble of the ATV, but they weren't afraid. They didn't run away.

"I see why you don't have a tan," she said flatly, "why you're never around until mid-afternoon. You're out here at night, like them."

Cal shifted into low gear and moved within 50 meters of the central group, composed of a large male and five females.

Then he froze them with the jacklight. The huge male could have been the same boomer they'd seen before: shaggy hair, his sex heavy between his muscular loins.

"You know how to handle that thing?" he asked when she'd pulled the weapon from the case. "That's an old-fashioned rifle you got there. No laserscope or anything."

Swinging its barrel through the windshield space, she pulled the Mauser up to her shoulder and smelled gun oil. "I took lessons in Wyoming. I'm an old-fashioned kind of girl."

"Whoa … That's the bull you're aimin' at. You'll spook the whole herd."

She squeezed the trigger gently, exhilarated, blinked when something in the crosshairs shimmered. Then the ATV cab filled with noise and 50 meters away a kangaroo slammed backward, stood erect one last time, and folded to the ground.

Val pulled the rifle down with a flush of success. The rest of the kangaroos took off with great graceful jumps. She caught a flash of red.

"You missed 'em. You got yourself the flyer behind 'em."

"What?"

"Give you a good skin, though. I could never hit anything with that damned thing either."

Val was numb with confusion. She shivered in the cool night air when they walked over, only then realized her skin was covered with a sheen of perspiration. Her mouth was dry.

The blue flyer was stone dead, her chest blown out. Something moved at her pouch, something small, smaller than her thumb. It was only the size of a mouse when it emerged, pink and hairless. The immature joey had arms and legs, articulated digits.

"Oh God."

"You wanna step on the skull," Cal said. "It's the best way. No chance it'd survive, see? You wanna be quick."

Its pink flesh was like gum rubber. She couldn't do it—when she turned away her stomach burned with pain.

In the still of the night, she heard a sound like the crushing of an eggshell.

◇

She was back at her wing of the hotel by one-thirty in the morning. In the end, she'd been saved from her sexual promise to Cal by a fluke: the alarm on his pager had gone off, and he'd just had time to drop her at the foyer before he drove off into the night. A night clerk's leer, for which she might have slapped him two days ago, now seemed hopelessly innocent.

How terribly everything had turned out.

Perhaps she could make a pet of Nell, perhaps Dr. Levich could drug the animal to make it tractable, perhaps Val could take it to New York and…

But once in her room, she understood that nothing was going to work out, not for the cowboy, not for Nell, not for her. She couldn't get the smell of gun oil off her hands. Her scattered clothes and half-packed bags—her plane was scheduled to leave the next day at noon—seemed to mirror her psychic disrepair. When she tried to pack she found herself stationary at the foot of the bed, grasping lingerie in one hand, her boots in the other, weeping.

She finally knelt against the mattress and slowly twisted into a fetal position. She lay on her side that way, shivering for ten minutes, before she fell asleep.

When the siren wailed two hours later and the helicopters shook the heavy glass doors along the garden she was so disoriented that at first she thought she was in New York, at Kenneth's apartment uptown, in the big bed. The rustic nightstand made her realize she was in Cabo; then the depths of sleep from which she was ascending suggested that she had just come awake from a dream, that the hunting trip with Cal had been a dream. But in the moonlight flooding the room she saw her dusty boots and bloody blouse, her scattered bags.

Past the sliding doors she could hear a raised voice, saw a shifting figure—a young man ran across the garden straight towards the foothills. A shaft of halogen white swept through the BioRange complex like an NYPD pass over Central Park West.

She remembered Nell in her stall.

She dressed quickly and ran down the walk past the mimosa trees, past the pool, through the lobby, through the other wing and past surgery along the gravel path to Nursery C. Just above the hills the inversion layer had moved closer to the resort, a low bank of clouds to the north, rolling like a wave on a long reef. A piece of heavy equipment ground overland away from the service road; one helicopter without lights flew so low that she was pushed sideways by its downdraft.

Lights were on in the nursery. The building door hung open. Its clinic rooms and hallways were empty, as if they had just been vacated.

And Nell was not in her enclosure. None of the animals were. Valerie fumbled with the lock to her stall, stumbled in and steadied herself in the straw. Her heart was pounding: the air was rich with the odors of dung and grass, hot with silence. She felt a draft of cooler night air—the outside gate to the exercise pen was open. She bent over and pushed through.

In the exercise yard, in the moonlight, what she saw seemed at first a jumble of dream images, some trick of perspective. Kangaroos were leaping over the fence. They were narrow-shouldered blues, fifteen, sixteen of them. She thought she saw Nell's smoky blue tail among them. The animals were circling, running along the fence, gathering speed, vaulting over the fence without effort. Val stumbled forward—then shrank back when she saw three boomers cornered at the far end of the pen. They were big, rust-colored with white faces, had to be from the hills since there'd been none in the nursery. One of them was smeared with blood.

They were squaring off, fighting the staff. The Latino veterinary nurse with the mustache lay disemboweled along the fence, his intestines glistening wet plum and black in the moonlight. Over the fence with graceful leaps blue flyers soared one by one: pregnant females were escaping.

Dr. Levich was screaming, "Hold your fire."

The blue flyers were running off with the children.

One of the women who'd been with Kai was holding her knee, gesturing at the hillside.

Cal's ATV was there, its jacklights bouncing as he turned in concert with a helicopter's spotlight—but the animal they sought would not quite freeze.

On the hilltop stood a large female with a scarred body. Out of her pouch protruded ... a filthy face, streaked and blemished. It was not a joey's face, but the unmistakably human face of a feral child of three or four, a boy or a girl, its hair long and matted.

It was the face of a human child.

Its shoulders came out of the pouch now—as if it was being born—its small hands clenched into waving fists.

THE GRATEFUL DEAD

Let's talk of graves, of worms and epitaphs.
— *Shakespeare*

Though the dead forget their dead in the House of Death,
I will remember, even there, my dear companion.
— *Homer, Iliad XXII*

I

We were just sitting there in the boardroom, Max and I, our black Italian wingtips propped up at one end of the long slate table, our backs sunk into charcoal velour. We were watching the Obituary Channel scroll by on the wallscreen. That's really when it all began: during one of those moments of stasis which originates a seminal, life-altering sequence of events, an otherwise preternaturally calm patch of time in which the tiniest seed of chaos fractalizes into a full-blown reordering of the cosmos. It goes without saying that what happened from this quiet beginning unalterably changed my life. It changed yours, too, I apologize to admit, as you will recognize once you fully understand what I am revealing now, publicly, for the first time.

To the industry, watching the Obits scroll by is "trolling." Different-sized vessels troll for different catches: the small firms troll for individual clients, those recently deceased for whom the mauve icon in the encoded rainbow of the color bar across the top of the screen indicates a still-open service contract. On our level—GD Inc. has six hundred franchised Homes nationwide and operations in Canada, Mexico, and Korea—we're more interested in demographic shifts, tracking market share, the kinds of data indicated by the shape of the color bar itself, its waves and fluctuations.

We started doing business even before "Elliott Anderson's Obituary Channel" was first bounced down from a satellite. Our genesis lay in the demise of the 20th century "baby boomer" generation, followed by the twin pandemics. As those populations died off, the demand for funerals increased exponentially, and the deathcare industry grew like bread rising under the action of yeast. We were the first chain to go interstate, the first to use CDC statistics to locate new Homes, the first with group plans (beginning with our benchmark contract with AARP). We shaped the franchise system of funeral homes you see today. So when Max minded the boardroom wallscreen, he eyed it with a proprietary air, like an institutional investor watching the big board dance before his or her eyes.

I confess I wasn't paying attention. I was staring past the wallscreen through our eightieth floor window at the mustard-colored atmosphere of downtown LA, wondering whether or not I was going to be able to sight Object 21/3847—a new comet, just named *Virgilius Maro*—as it finally hove into earth's sight next week. My hobby is imaging astronomical objects with HD++ clarifying video. I was concluding that the only way I was going to be able to see *V. Maro* for the full fourteen seconds it would take for me to properly capture its image was by leasing space on Mauna Kea. This gave new meaning to the phrase "visible to the naked eye."

"Pass the fucking embalming fluid," Max growled. "They're killin' us."

"Mmmm. Us?"

He pointed at a new symbol, an ideograph, showing up in the color bar of the Obit Channel screen. "Like who's this new outfit, Ancestors?"

"Asian specialists. Headquartered in Beijing," I said,

stretching, sitting up. At least I'd been keeping up with *Post Mortem,* our trade magazine. "They started out as All Friends Mortuary Society. Special noodle feature on all banquet menus, monk's food, saffron theme. Niche market. Specials include ancestors appear in holocube..."

"They're not the only ones."

"C'mon, Max. We're still doing close to three billion a year."

Max took a deep breath, rubbed his eyes, and spoke softly. "Not anymore. Two-eight is what we billed last year. This year we thought two-six. Now look at the way the market's turned on us. We'll be lucky to hurdle one-five."

"Really?"

"Your head's been in the clouds, Coop. Ever since Harriet took off last year."

"I am reading the trades." I could feel myself blush. My divorce aside, the truth is, the business end of things had never seized me the way it had Max—a business which, I recalled with a pang of guilt, had treated me very well (ask Harriet, whose settlement included a condo *complex* in Cabo). Lately I had been acting like the numbers had little to do with me.

"We were the first with drive-through viewing," Max said, "the first with unit pricing, the first with mobile embalming centers..."

My implanted pager hummed against my heart. I used the excuse to ease myself out of my chair. "Cheer up," I said without conviction. "We'll think of something."

"Well, you're the artist, Coop," Max said with a crooked grin. "Right?"

◇

Right, I suppose. I started out as a videographer, got into deathcare by scanning in sample make-up treatments on a part-time basis for Max when he was still Sczyczypek Family Funeral Home. I stuck with Max when the business took off. It was I who unified the company image with the Angel® theme when we went national, I who selected the Mozart

Requiem® as the signature for our international line. It was I who designed our logo, the gilt letters G and D surrounded by a gold, O-shaped frame, spelling in an oblique way a sacred three-letter word to those of our customers who wanted reassurance that they'd chosen the right provider in their time of need.

My only disagreement with Max had been over the name change, from Sczyczypek to Grateful Dead. Not that I didn't think Sczyczypek couldn't be improved upon, but how could the dead—let me call your attention to the operative noun here—be Grateful®? Oh, I know the history of the term, its use by a 20th century rock group; its source as a descriptive term for a British ballad in which a human helps a ghost find peace. But we're talking about corpses here, not ghosts. Max pursued the fiction of their satisfaction as our trademark marketing strategy. Another one of our signatures became the Mona Lisa® smile on the face of each of our clients. (True, I was the one who fabricated the mold for the plastic insert—who was I to argue with success?) But aside from giving the franchise its name, Max mostly stuck to the books and left the rest to me.

Which meant that I was the one who was paged that morning. I had a warrantee problem to deal with.

In the previous month the Westwood Grateful Dead had cremated the remains of a prominent judge. His widow had called the Westwood facility to report that the urn containing her husband's ashes had been—stay with me here—making noises. I mean producing sounds: creaks, pops, strings of rapid ticks, little noises like that. The Westwood unit had sent their man out, but he'd come back baffled. They'd kicked the problem up to the franchise level, where it bounced over to me.

You may already know me well enough to know that I prefer to work away from the boardroom. Yet that day the relief I felt in walking away from Max's news was balanced by a chill that ran down my spine when I identified the gray cast I'd been seeing over our flotilla of maglev Fleetwoods in the motor pool, limos whose paint usually gleamed so black they shimmered in the light. They'd started looking like funereal battleships.

I hadn't understood what was turning them that color: they were gathering dust.

◇

It took me twenty minutes to drive to Westwood.

I found a pastel mansion at the address, all flat planes and glass walls. When I activated the residential scanner the door was answered by a tall, leggy blonde in a microskirt, hair all frizzed out, green lipstick. "I'm her niece," she said, then promptly disappeared.

She left a rich cinnamon odor in the air.

Then Keiko MacPhee appeared in the foyer, dressed in black. She was younger than I'd expected, thin but sturdy, with dark eyes and full lips. Her long hair was pulled back in an austere way. I was struck by the way I could see her bones beneath the spare flesh of her shoulders, her forearms, her long elegant fingers, as if her mortality lay waiting just beneath her skin. Which of course it did. I found her very attractive.

"I'm Cooper Boyd," I said. "From GD Inc."

"This way," she said, turning and pulling me in her wake into a living room with a vaulted ceiling, faux rustic furniture, and a stark stone fireplace, a tribal hearth in the Nomad style that's been so big for the past few years. I recognized the pyramid set like a trophy in the center of the rough mantel as a customized Model 986 Solid Titanium Urn, our finest unit —a phoenix sculpted in bas-relief on its front.

The leggy blonde slipped through the room, now with a jacket over her shoulder, pecking her aunt on the cheek. "Back about midnight," she said. Then she smiled at me through her green lipstick. "My name's Unix. Nice suit."

"Italian," I assented, pleased. I watched her leave. "Mrs. MacPhee," I said, turning my attention back to the widow, "you don't look old enough to be her aunt. And yet the judge . . ."

"… was a hundred and seventeen when he died. I'm … thirty-nine. The judge spent a lot of money on life extension. And the dear man, he insisted on spending some on me."

We made small talk about adjusting to the loss of a loved one, about the house, about the noise she'd been hearing. Judge MacPhee, I confirmed, was the elderly gentleman in the nearby holopix. Big ears, a rapacious smile, the red and white plaid pants only judges can wear with impunity. Mrs. MacPhee—call me Keiko, she insisted—explained with quiet intelligence how the judge, whom she'd met clerking out of law school, had died during his third artificial heart installation. She'd had him cremated on his instructions, against her own wishes for cryogenic preservation in an elaborate home sarcophagus offered by one of our competitors.

Above the low hum of the house's climate control, I was startled to hear a pop that definitely seemed to have come from the urn; it was followed by a long, low whistle, mournful and remote.

Keiko shivered. "It's… Now he's started doing that."

When I looked at her in silence, she sighed.

"Oh, I understand," she said. "Those are only ashes and an urn."

"Cremation is very conclusive," I nodded slowly. She'd beaten me to where I had come to try, for her own good, to take her. I admired her good sense. "So there's probably a fairly…"

"… pedestrian explanation," she completed my sentence. She took a deep breath. "I'm trying to live with that. What I can't live with," she said, smiling wryly, "is a noisy urn." She looked away. "I loved him dearly. It's like he's still here somehow."

The urn made another pop. Keiko and I stood together in the ensuing silence and raised eyebrows at each other, then she looked away again. There was a sensuous quality to the way she filled out her dress, to her scent, to the way she worked her lower lip with her teeth.

I inspected the unit, which appeared to be capable of

surviving its three-hundred-year warrantee: terrific heft, perfect seams, that quality anodized titanium finish. "I'll take it in," I suggested. "Do some scans, replace the urn, see what happens." I pictured myself returning the unit personally.

"I'd be grateful," she said. "I'm sure you understand. How can I let go?" She sighed, then bit her lower lip. "When you come back, come for dinner."

"I'll call you just as soon as I know something," I said, my heart flooding with joy.

◇

I stopped by Max's spread in Santa Monica. I'd been avoiding my own home since Harriet left. I set my Lotus on auto-park and ducked in the kitchen door after acknowledging the residential scanner. I was whistling as I walked into the den.

Max's son Lance—a pudgy kid, pale as a mushroom—was home on spring break from Caltech. He was as smart as his dad was savvy, but to Max's dismay he was utterly indifferent to the funeral business. Max had no other kids.

"Well, you're happy," Lance said, looking up from the green glow of a holocube game he'd reconfigured. "Did you see your comet?"

"Something like that." I smiled, realizing that I'd forgotten my sighting problems, forgotten the problems at work.

"Maybe you can cheer up dad. He's really a case."

"Never fucking mind," Max said as he shuffled into the room. He was already wearing his bathrobe, a bad sign.

"What happened?" I asked.

"We lost the regional contract for Triple A."

There goes all that holiday business, passed through my mind. *There goes 500 mill. There goes 1-800-FATALITY.* I cleared my throat, tried at least to speak positively. "Max, you know, when we started, there were eight billion people on the planet. Now there are sixteen. I don't care what contract we lose, potentially…"

"What do you want us to do, start bumping people off?" Max had migrated to his bar, behind which hung my videograph of a slowly rotating Jupiter. He poured himself a tumbler of the green Japanese melon liquor he favored. "We need a new idea. Something big."

I was thinking about Keiko and her niece, about her late husband, about life extension. "Immortality," I mused.

"What?" Lance said.

I paused. "Convince the market that you can provide clients some way to live forever."

"We *had* a plan once," Max told Lance, his face crinkling with a memory from our early days, and now I remembered too, to my embarrassment. "We planned to holotape people," Max told his son, "You know, like a presentation thing about them, THIS IS YOUR LIFE, they signed on when they were alive. Once they died, we'd broadcast the tape on the anniversary of their deaths. The idea was, we'd beam it down from a satellite on Fox, say, or Disney, or Fiat. Like during halftimes, or even in commercial slots. It was perpetual care, see? Every year you'd come back. We called it IMMORTALITY NOW!"

"Cool," Lance said. "Technology's a little dated, but still..."

"A holographic eternal flame; electrons and photons dancing to the virtual reincarnation of your self..." I quoted from the brochure we'd worked up.

"Very cool," Lance said. "There's your lost market share."

Max's eyes gleamed. "Market share? Did you hear this kid? Market share?"

"I like the technology, dad," Lance blushed. "Why didn't you run the program, Uncle Coop?"

I took a deep breath. "Didn't cost out. You sell broadcast in perpetuity, how do you support all that transponder time, Obit Channel fees, all that? Turns out we'd need our own satellite, permits from the UN Space Agency, production facilities, all that for starters, just to make a go of it. Your dad worked out the figures."

Lance scrunched up his nose. "Maybe if you tweaked the hardware..."

Max was beaming at him. But in the end, I knew he was going to have to admit to his son that the idea didn't go anywhere. I thought I'd spare myself the unpleasant part. "Busy morning tomorrow," I said. "I'm out of here."

◇

Max wasn't at the office when I drove in the next morning, which I took to be a good sign—why take our reverses so seriously? We'd earned our dollar. So what could we do? By giving up on everything else, I was able to concentrate on my class.

I teach the franchisees what we in the business call "setting features." The corpses that come to us often stare up from their gurneys, eyes wide and mouths agape, cheeks slack from gravity. Our service is to make them look dead, not actually dead, transfixed with the abyss or vacant-eyed as cooked lobsters, but properly, conventionally dead. So we shave them, close their eyes, their mouths, shut the openings that in life were ever active: we set the features. We fold the hands, one over the other, over the umbilicus: a posture of repose, peace with dignity at last. The final detail, here at GD, is insertion and adjustment of the Mona Lisa® smile.

The fitting comes in seven sizes.

It's a serene time for me, passing from corpse to corpse among the Angels® on the walls, Mozart's Requiem® in the air, murmuring with the students, seeing peace drive out fright on the faces below my hands.

About eleven I got back to my office and was able to start on the urn. It looked seamless, but a magnetic lock inside the Model 986 responds to a proprietary magnetic key and the pyramid unfolds into four triangles.

The judge's ashes were intact in a traditional Ziploc bag: a generous cup of fine white and tan powder, bone fragments and white chunks, a couple the size of stream pebbles. Although we burn at 4500 degrees, not every part of the body vaporizes, and some of the body's bones—the pelvis, for example—are so large as to resist reduction. Still, the total mass only came to seven point four ounces, a handful of dust. It is instructive how little even the rich and powerful come to, in the end.

I spread the ashes on a lab table for inspection. One bone fragment reminded me strongly of the new Matsushita turtle logo, but that was about it. I ran a series of scans on the urn's inner sleeve, came up with nothing. I tried heating and cooling the unit and listened for thermal flex noises. Nothing again. I delaminated the phoenix, sent each stratum through computer-aided tomography. Nada. What the hell was going on?

◇

I took my lunch up to the boardroom, brought an extra corned beef sandwich, spread it out on the slate table—but Max still wasn't around. His wife, Dorothy, didn't know where he was either; I supposed he was worrying the bean counters on the twenty-fourth floor.

Morosely, I ate and watched the Obit Channel. Our GD logo continued to shrink as our market share fell. When I looked away, out the window, the atmosphere was socked in again, this time with a browner cast to it, like the mustard had gone bad; you couldn't remotely see the heavens; you'd have trouble frame grabbing a streetlight tonight.

Then late in the afternoon, using a stereo zoom technique from cosmic body imaging, I finally discovered an anomaly in the ashes: a tiny green drop, shiny, like a fused gemstone. Its hardness registered in the diamond range and its translucent surface, like Chinese jade, offered no clue to its interior. I thought I could make out a minuscule rectangle of shaded stripes, but it might have been my imagination.

Then I heard the little bugger creak.

I called Keiko who toggled on video when she recognized my voice. She was wearing navy blue today, which suggested an advance in her grieving process. I told her what I'd found.

"Did the judge have any gems on his person, any implants, anything like that?"

"No implants that weren't recycled. Do you think you've solved the problem?"

"Once I figure out what this green thing is..."

◇

My efforts were interrupted by a message from Max asking me to cover a business meeting. I still couldn't find Max himself—but since he knew how I hated taking meetings, I was hardly surprised.

Keesha, Max's secretary, gave me a wink of conspiratorial approval when she ushered in the sales rep, an ancient gnome with the unlikely name of Slaughter.

The salesman represented a line of containers suitable for the cremates of family pets. They looked like stuffed animals, fluffy birds and cats and fish with big eyes, had microprocessors inside and made lifelike twitches for months on a tiny rechargeable. "Max said you needed to work on your numbers," Mr. Slaughter said with a wet smile.

Has it come to this? I asked myself. True, when my black Lab Balthazar died, on the way back from the crematorium I'd wound up shoving his ashes into the glovebox of my Lotus, where they'd stayed for want of a proper spot. *Maybe a full-service franchise should have something for everybody* passed through my mind. But this was going too far.

I ran Mr. Slaughter out. Keesha gave me the evil eye. "It's not like we don't have a problem," she hissed.

As for the little green thing, I kept thinking chip, though I'd never seen anything quite like it. At noon the next day, I finally found Max. Inadvertently. I was tracking down Lance to help me identify the green blob. I found my call forwarded from Lance's holocube game to a lab at Caltech in Pasadena.

"It may be the remains of one of those new biochips," Lance said after a moment's study on the vidphone. "Looks fried. You can still read the barcode, though... Huh. Lemme scan this..."

The vidphone screen was suddenly taken up by Max's face, bushy eyebrows wagging. He looked manic. "We're back in business," he shouted.

"What are you talking about?"

Max pushed Lance back in front of the camera sensor. Lance was blushing. "You're the one who gave us the idea, Uncle Coop," Lance said. "It started with your comet."

"What about my comet? What idea?"

"We're using *Virgilius Maro* to produce the signal we need for IMMORTALITY NOW! I've been taking courses in radio astronomy this semester. Did you know comets and their tails move through the solar system like huge generators?" He waved his hands around. "They come slicing through the system with a bigtime surge of radio frequency signals we get as broadband noise. I mean, comets produce it, generate radio frequency signals, in a major way. It's, like, the snow between channels?"

"Yes," I said, vaguely familiar through radio imaging. "And?"

"All we need to do is organize that RF noise and transform it into something useful—our image carrier, say. Digitalize it, modulate it with the holounits you want broadcast... Then you send *back* to the comet a one-time countersignal to reshape the original RF noise into the signal you want broadcast. Bingo..."

"Bingo?"

"Bingo. You've got a customized signal that'll be transmitted through the solar system on every pass of the comet until, uh ... ten to the seventh over pi ... for about, uh, four hundred million years?"

"You're not seriously ... Max?"

There was his face again, shiny with perspiration, beatific with a kind of madness.

"Look, Max," I said, "It's nice to have Lance in the loop here, but aren't we reaching a bit? Selling radio noise from a comet? Isn't that a little out of our range?"

Max's grin might have been shaped by a Mona Lisa® insert. "Not like we have a choice, Coop."

"It's O'Donald's, Uncle Coop," Lance said off camera.

I saw Max wince. He was particularly touchy about the mortuary arm of McDonald's Corp., the O'Donald's chain. "Those cheap maggots," Max said grimly, "with their fake Irish Wakes and that stupid fucking clown, Digger O'Donald."

"What did they do?"

"They underbid us for the AARP contract."

Now it was my turn to wince. Perhaps we were finished after all. No business can downsize by half overnight and not experience disaster. I looked up. The Angels® on the wall seemed surprised too. I noticed a film of dust on *their* wings; were we already laying off maintenance staff up here in the suites as well?

The monitor framed the faces of both Max and his son: the Earth and the Moon, Jupiter and Io. I imagined retiring into another life with a woman like Keiko, working through the night somewhere, frame grabbing shooting stars. How nice it would be to have that kind of human satisfaction when the business was coming down—a son you loved, a loyal wife. "You guys do what you want," I said. "We're due for some luck." I was certain, of course, that our luck had run out.

"Send me the chip!" Lance blurted out under a squeeze from his dad.

II

"A memory chip?" Keiko said.

"Apparently it survived the cremation, so it's clearly some hardened circuit. Maybe part of a life-extension implant that didn't melt down, maybe something else..."

She was sitting across from me at Espagio's. Its aquarium wall bubbled behind her in an algae-laden homage to Venice, the Italian city which had sunk just the year before to rising sea levels. Keiko's niece Unix had suggested the place, winking at me in a way which, I felt, boosted my stock. I'd needed the boost; the news about her husband's remains had changed

Keiko. She'd put more holopix of the judge around the house and she was wearing black again. She seemed drawn into herself.

"Is the chip readable?"

I recited again the printout of the message text Lance had sent me that morning. "Bubble memory nano chip exchanging gasses through a quantum field. Proprietary barcode, unlisted, bio range."

"Bio range. I haven't been able stop thinking about that."

I folded the mostly blank paper down to a sixth its size, the proportions of a coffin. "All of us wait for signals from the dead," I told her. "We watch for signs that they're still there, listen for voices to tell us that they still care. People are even happy when we hear that some deceased soul has done some outrageous thing, like disappeared from a grave or sat up in a coffin or made noise from an urn. As if any of that proves they're much like the living and that we're still on *their* minds. You have to be realistic, Keiko."

"Do you know I'm really *fifty-nine*?" she said quietly. "He was a bastard to a lot of people. But not to me."

I'd guessed fifty; not bad. "Mrs. MacPhee. Keiko..."

"First the noises, now this chip. It would be like him to leave something. Maybe he's just saying hello. Maybe..." She sighed, looking away with dark eyes that mixed sadness and hope.

Well, the surprise was on me. Life always turns out to be more complex than you'd planned for it to be. I'd only just figured out what I really wanted in life—the love of a woman like Keiko, a life together to complete my own approaching sixties—and now here I was, the rival of a bag of ashes. And losing. I put my two hands over hers on the center of the table, nudging aside my plate, felt a tremor in my palm. "Maybe you ought to get out more," I said, deciding to go for it. "Unix told me that you've been alone in your house since ... Go for a walk. Anywhere, to a park. Dig around in your garden." Embarrassed, I felt my face go hot and I muttered, "Have um, a fling."

She smiled.

"Well, it would be a mistake to give you hope about the judge."

"I suppose you must be right. But until I really know about this chip…"

"Give me a couple more days. Just don't expect a miracle. The only *real* miracle is …" I said, waving my arms, "all round you." I'd intended to wave at life itself, but I found myself waving at replica Espagio's, at the movie people at the tables, at Unix, coming in the blue-green glass door, a head-turner in her short reflective dress.

Still, my strategy with Keiko seemed to be working. As I helped her into Unix's van at the curb she let her hand linger in mine and smiled. "My niece was right about you," she said. "You're a lot of fun."

At breakfast the next morning I found myself watching an infomercial on the Obit Channel whose strangely familiar elements took a long time for me to fully recognize.

The screen had gone European with archaic reds and blues and golds, morphed into an ersatz ancient tapestry whose vague robed figures came to life holding hands and ascending through some sort of stagy empyrean busy with GD Angels®. A smooth, deep voice intoned: "Star with saints and heroes in a dazzling holographic celebration your descendants will cherish forever. Travel through eternity clothed in the authentic finery of medieval Florence…"

I recognized the voice from an ad for our International Line. Medieval Florence? The hair on the back of my neck stood up. What I was looking at was an infomercial for IMMORTALITY NOW!

I was even partly responsible for it. When we'd kicked around the idea years ago I'd suggested holotaping the clients (or, failing their actual presence, their AI-generated images) in scenes set in the ascending circles of Paradise as imagined by Dante Alighieri. I mean, it had been just an idea. Now apparently Max had gotten someone to develop it.

I paged the rest of the executive floor for Max, got forwarded to Pasadena.

"We're getting great results," Lance told me enthusiastically from the Caltech lab. Max, who appeared disheveled, was behind him, teleconferencing with a bank of monitors; I recognized the rainbow colors of the GD Regional Franchisee Net. "Fantastic results," Lance went on. "A friend of mine from the radio astronomy club has an internship at the SETI transmitter in Arecibo, Puerto Rico. We're working with him. Dad leased the site for the duration."

"Arecibo? The whole site?"

"We're going for a burst transmission on the 31st," Lance gushed.

Max had migrated to the vidphone and joked about buying down the national debt with the deal for Arecibo.

"Cripes," Lance said, "are we getting bandwidth! We'll be able to encode enough information to broadcast tactile holography in a window of about eight hours real time. Then with compression ... We're trying to squeeze in a full twenty-four-hour day."

"I still don't get it," I said, trying to stay calm. "How does this signal override all the other signals people get?"

"The way sunspots affect even hardened satellites; you fiddle with the magnetosphere a bit. *Virgilius Maro*'s that big, and we punch him up besides. Terrific lot of RF noise. Now if Virgil was just a little closer to earth, ha ha."

There was Max over his shoulder, munching popcorn. "Isn't it great how Lance's finally taken an interest in the business?" Max said. "It's been a dream, to pass it on to the kid: *Sczyczypek* forever. Wait till you see the spots we've got running on the Obit Channel."

"Max, that's what I called you about."

"Virgil, everybody's calling the comet Virgil, don't you love it? How could we pass the Dante angle up? I know you usually handle the art director end of things, but how you've been lately... I thought I'd turn it over to Fiat/Disney."

"Max..."

"It's a business decision, Coop." The way Max tensed his jaw when he spoke, that distant look in his eyes, reminded me that it was, after all, his business. I held my tongue. Anyway, I thought, who wants to paint the hull of a sinking ship?

"We're already selling units," he went on. "From six this morning we've had a lease on reference studio space in the Valley. We'll have virtual setups in every franchise city by week's end. Overnight we've sold sixty thousand slots of that *Paradiso* so far—hey, you think that's too Italian? ParadiseLand maybe?"

Max downloaded other segments of the advertising program into a window on my wallscreen and I saw more of Fiat/Disney's work, even one of the holounits themselves. Now I knew what those high production levels, those make-up jobs reminded me of: a soap opera. Set in Thirteenth-Century Florence, laced with special effects, but soap opera all the same. It was painful to watch. I felt the way any writer feels when a story of his or hers is worked over, distorted. I felt surrounded by disaster.

It had been a good run, with the company, I found myself thinking.

"Don't look so glum, Uncle Coop." Lance seemed a little embarrassed himself. "I got something else on the chip. Set of chips, I guess we should say. Apparently the, uh, cooking it went through? Thermal conversion auto-booted a runnable file to access mass storage? Or at least so say the probes. Amazing how the lines hold up. I think I got the power leads identified to the CPU and the bubble memory. Who knows, I might even be able to run that sucker. Or ruin it for good. I mean, it's really a longshot."

"Do what you can," I smiled automatically, but the room really began to swim around me now. Destroy it! I wanted to shout. Give it to me! *I'll* ruin it. I had just been comforting myself with a vision of retirement with Keiko and my rival's dust refused to settle, if you know what I mean.

After I hung up different schemes passed through my mind. Get it back from Lance, send it down the trash chute, flush it down the john. But gradually, after twenty minutes of controlled breathing, I settled down.

I did have qualms of conscience about destroying it, after all. And I was curious about what would happen if Lance tried to run the program ("*ruin it for good,*" ran through my mind). Still, I resolved to withhold this latest development from Keiko. I would tell her that we hadn't made any progress, that it looked like there was nothing to the chip after all.

As the comet approached, I could lose myself in setting up the imaging equipment, dirty though the atmosphere continued to be. I'd planned to invite Keiko to drive down to Baja with me, but word was even Baja was socked in. So I would have to console myself with beta-testing new Zeiss filters; they were ingenious: including power supply, the whole set fit into the palm of my hand.

My specialty is the suitcase-sized observatory. There is a special pleasure in handling such fine equipment, calibrating the sensors, cleaning the lenses, inputting the current project's program, coordinating frame-action with celestial coordinates, running through simulations whose successes and failures both leave you hanging, peacefully and without messy human contact, somewhere among the stars.

The comet was a big event in the news: icy infalling interstellar material from the Kuiper Belt, a remnant of the formation of the solar system. The best estimate of its mass was a bit over a hundred kilotons, the size of a small mountain, a fairly rare event. A comet that big, impacting the Earth, would cause an untold catastrophe, its energy yield on the order of 20,000 megatons, equivalent to all the nuclear weapons produced in the previous century. But though *V. Maro*'s 272 year orbit would be close in cosmic terms, no measurable effect to earth was expected beyond an interruption in communications, and an incredible show.

◇

The latest data on *Virgilius Maro*—which everyone was calling Virgil now—was everywhere. It was on CNN, VNN, running as an occasional window on the Obit Channel.

A comet-related story was running on the wallscreen at Keiko's house the next evening when I arrived for my promised dinner, the titanium urn and what remained of the judge's ashes in my hands. Yes, I'd told Keiko that the chip inquiry had come to a dead end.

I was feverish with guilt and lust.

Unix, wearing a silver microdress decorated with signs of the Zodiac, met me at the door and took the urn from my hands. She set it on the foyer table. "Aunt Keiko's instructions," she said. "She's taking your advice about burying the ashes and the urn in a regular grave. Burying what's left of Uncle—my *dad*'s uncle, actually. Still, she's been like an aunt to me."

"I'm just trying to make her happy," I said.

"I can tell." she smiled. "She's out back..."

I found Keiko outside in the neglected kitchen garden, hands dirty but cheerful. She was filling pots with soil.

"Not much bigger than this," she said, holding up a parsley seed. I realized she was talking about the chip. "Nothing to it, then?"

"No," I said. "Nothing at all. My technician still has the chip, but your husband's ashes are otherwise intact. I wasn't sure you wanted the, uh, since... No noises anymore."

She shrugged. "Something from an implant then, after all," she said, shaking her head. She drained her glass of vodka. "Now let's have dinner. I've got a fifty-year-old bottle of wine."

Afterwards, we sat by a fire in the living room, drank port and watched a bit of the comet special on VNN. Unix settled in with us. She'd had a falling out with her boyfriend.

The special was interrupted, to my dismay, by a commercial for IMMORTALITY NOW! from Grateful Dead. Elderly men and women romped around a fountain in a cobbled square—Max had turned creative control entirely over to Fiat/Disney.

The little cartoon animals splashing in the water of the fountain, the voiceover sales pitch, the promise of a *Purgatorio* sequel, made me burn with shame.

The tacky part, though, cheered up Unix, and she cheered me up, and we started to chat, sunk so happily in the sofa by the Nomad firehearth that I didn't at first realize that Keiko had been out of the room for some time.

Unix blushed a little, smiled, and disappeared.

It was getting late, and I wasn't sure what to do. Then the lights dimmed, and I thought I saw someone in the hallway to the master suite at the rear of the house, hand raised at about the level of a console for a house computer. A moment later subdued harp music floated through the air. Then Keiko walked slowly into the room wearing a black silk robe.

She stopped at the hearth, her hands resting on the slate platform, fingers splayed, her hair down around her shoulders, the fire reflected on her face. She had continued drinking—I could see it in her eyes, in her breathing, in the way she swayed, ever so slightly. I calculated the time since the judge had been cremated: a month, exactly. The grieving process takes different forms for different people; I had used my professional experience to read her precisely.

"The kind of man he was, my late husband," she said. "He would have wanted me to jump back in. You're that kind of man too."

I cleared my throat. Would you believe me if I told you that I realized then that what I had encouraged in her was wrong, that things between us had moved too fast, that for her own good I was going to turn her down, hug her gently and lead her back to her bed and tuck her in and tell her to go to sleep? I'm not sure I believe myself either. Oh, I realized I'd been wrong, certainly, but the way she'd said *jump back in* I'd fallen completely, victim to my desires, victim to the silky curve at her waist, to the huskiness in her voice.

Keiko and Unix, forgive me.

As it was, I was saved by my pager, which hummed against my heart insistently.

The message was from Lance, He was paging me from the mortuary lab in the basement of the GD tower. The message read: Highest Urgency.

◇

When I found him, Lance was crouched over a jury-rigged assembly surrounded by a bank of instruments—I recognized a light-enhancing stereo microscope.

"You'll never know what ecstasy you interrupted," I said dryly.

"Uncle Coop," Lance said, pointing to an eyepiece. "Look at this."

I put the bridge of my nose between the soft cups of rubber. At first I didn't see anything but a mottled background, then discerned what seemed an aberration, a comic little figure, a smaller grid of red and white.

"You may not believe me at first," Lance said, his voice tight with excitement, "but I think that's the Judge. Or some manifestation of him, like a homunculus. It was created by the chipset when I powered it up... See, first thing it did was output a nutrient program, carbon high. I used my Pepsi. Next thing I knew... See, it was a sequence, started with the sound chip, to call attention to itself..."

"Christ!" I said. "It's a little person. Those are plaid pants."

I continued to watch the figure in wonder as Lance brought me up to speed. The judge had bought into a duplication technology, he told me. "There's a DNA info base in nano memory, quark based, really something. Then a generator that kicks in when that program runs, comes out of a lot of compression. Well, he reproduces himself, see? This guy actually figured out a way to live forever."

"Guy? What do you mean, guy? This is some kind of bacteria."

"Yeah, that's true, right," Lance said. "There's a bug in the scalar routine?"

"Scalar routine?"

"Formally it's the function of two vectors, equal to the

product of their magnitudes and the cosine of the angle between them? Anyway, if you get the dot point wrong..."

"Lance, what are you talking about?"

"What went wrong. It's in the sequence for the scalar routine, what makes him this size. See, the chipset reproduced him all right, but the dot point got shifted. Got his scale wrong by a factor of one thousand. Poor sucker. I did the calculations. He's one one-thousandth the size of an actual man."

So there he was, my rival, who less than an hour ago, in the strange complicated way of human affairs, had interposed himself between me and the consummation of my dreams. Who, I asked myself, stood between me and my dreams now?

I started to laugh, but I swear I saw a tiny fist raised, shaking, directly at me.

I sucked in a deep breath. "I'd better contact Mrs. MacPhee immediately," I said, reaching for the vidphone.

III

That was the beginning of the week you all remember, the week that changed all our lives.

Later that Monday morning astronomers announced that *Virgilius Maro*'s course had unaccountably shifted. The large comet was now headed directly toward the planet Earth.

Impact was expected in seven days, fourteen hours, and six minutes.

I see I've barely touched upon the catastrophic possibilities impact presented, but I'm sure you remember some of them: how a comet *V. Maro*'s size had crashed into the Yucatan at the end of the Cetacean Era and ended the reign of the dinosaurs, how the current human casualty estimate ran into the billions. Alone in the glow of wallscreens and in groups from school auditoriums to cathedrals we contemplated the possibility of a conflagration that would produce rampant volcanism, sulfur clouds, an extended period of darkness, soaring temperatures followed by a new ice age, the extinction of species after species and eliminate most of the world's biomass. Scientists were scrambling to turn the comet off its course with a thermonuclear explosion in space. NASA ran twenty-four hour shifts, and the Chinese mobilized their "factory-in-space" program to produce a delivery vehicle loaded and launched from the UN Station. Nukes were being readied and shuttled up, but as there were only a few hundred left on the planet, NASA was having logistics problems, and the decision to go with the Ukrainian multiple warheads (the infamous "cabbage bombs") made everyone nervous. As well, as we all now know, we should have been.

As for Grateful Dead, Inc., the effect on the firm was paradoxical. With so much potential death on the way, suddenly lots of people wanted to make arrangements. They reasoned, and rightly so, that in the event of impact there would be a run on deathcare services, and that the average consumer would be best accommodated by the world-wide facilities of a full-service chain such as ours.

Just after the President's announcement, I finally found Max. He was up in the boardroom, sprawled in his captain's chair at the end of the long slate table, transfixed on the Obit Channel running full wallscreen on the other side of the room. His little fax dish had pulled in a library of invoices, printed out balance sheets and ledger pages, all heaped around him. On his laptop was loaded a draft page from the upcoming annual report to shareholders.

"Fuck the business," I told him. "Go home to your wife and son. Nobody really knows about this, nobody knows for sure we're safe until it's deflected." I was still shaken by the tic the President had developed halfway through his speech.

"Coop, we've completely sold out *Paradiso,*" Max said with barely controlled excitement. "It's damned amazing. *Purgatorio's* half committed as of an hour ago—*Purgatorio,* where clients gotta shuffle around these circle things admitting they ate too much or slept too much or whatever turned them on. Fiat/Disney's even working up an *Inferno* segment. We got couples buying adjoining units as gifts, we got groups who want to tape on the last day, like have a comet party and tape their segments."

"Max," I said, "all of us may only have a week to live. Don't you understand? The comet could hit the planet. Even a near miss..."

Max blushed red. "Yeah, yeah," he mumbled. "I'm no rocket scientist, but hey, Coop, I figure, it turned, it'll turn again, see?"

"How can you talk like that?"

Max pushed away from the table, got up, swung around and pulled his baggy suit coat off the back of the chair. He shoved his arm into a coat sleeve. "Gotta go. I got a presentation to give to FEMA. You wanna come? I know you're not up to speed these days, Coop, but I always feel better if you're there. Backup?"

"FEMA? Who's FEMA?"

"Federal Emergency Management. You know. We're cutting a deal on a pre-need thing. See, they got a mandated formula for disaster preparation. The front money on this one alone gets us back up over three bil. Ain't that ironic? Just when we get IMMORTALITY NOW! workin' better than expected? You dance for a drizzle, you get a hurricane. And look at you. Who am I to say you haven't been up to speed? Who gave us the comet?"

"Max, what's the fucking funeral business worth if the whole world ends? You may never have another night to bounce on your bed with Dorothy. You may never have another Monday afternoon to spend with Lance. Live a little, for Christ's sake."

As if on cue, Lance himself rushed in, his pale face flushed pink, waving a sheaf of figures that turned out to be estimates for the FEMA meetings. He told his father in clipped tones that they were going to be late if they didn't get going. Max jammed papers into his briefcase, folded his battered old computer, and the two of them ran off as I stood there, still scolding.

Even as I ranted on, I could see the error of my ways.

There Max had gone: busy with the company of his son, awash with business, fulfilled. Do you want to know how desperate *I* was? I tried to get in touch with Harriet. She has a new hyphenated name—no, not just a hyphenated last name, but a hyphenated first name as well. NuKiwi-Harriet Finney-Boyd. There's no going back at all in life, is there.

◇

At the request of Unix, I checked in on Keiko.

"How's your aunt taking it?" I asked in the foyer when she answered the door.

"She's doin' great. *She* is, anyway. You know, Coop, Aunt Keiko always went for those short-man-syndrome, power-trip guys. The Napoleonic types? I mean, really, now the judge is as short as you can get, right?"

I looked at her with surprise.

"I don't mean to disrespect Uncle," she said. "He's my father's favorite uncle; I do love him, and I'm glad that he's ... back, sort of back. But he's always been a real tyrant, little dictator bossing everybody around. Now he's even worse than he was before."

I laughed. "I don't mean to disrespect him either," I said, "but I could tell by the way he dressed."

"Myself, I prefer taller guys like you. Fewer insecurities."

I blushed. "Ah, Unix, I just wish I wasn't too old for you."

She giggled. "How old do you think I am?"

"Nineteen, at the outside," I told her.

"Try twenty-nine. Uncle bought a bunch of that life extension stuff for me too, bless him." She was wearing that tight green microskirt again, turned and walked away with a provocative wiggle. It is extraordinary how a bit of information can change your point of view.

The threat of the end of the world aside, I remember thinking then, *we live in wonderful times.*

◇

A miniature life-support unit, consisting of racks of

equipment sent over from GD Inc., and two exotic consoles from Switzerland, had been set up around a lab table in the living room, a nest of tubing and thin wires terminating in a light-enhancing stereo microscope. Keiko was there, apparently keeping a constant vigil. The judge had grown, but he was still quite small, inhabiting a heated area on a textured slide.

Keiko was a feverish specter. After I had politely put my eye to the microscope eyepiece for a moment she gave me her hand. An understanding had developed between us.

"How can he live like that?"

"He can't," she said. "His doctors tell us that he'll survive for seven days maximum."

"How tragic," I said, searching my professional vocabulary for the right thing to say.

"What's it matter?" a strange elderly voice said. I looked around me, startled. By the expressions on Keiko's and Unix's faces I realized we were listening to the judge; apparently his voice was picked up by sensors on the microscope stage and piped through the home quatro sound. His voice seemed to come from everywhere. The effect was eerie; my skin tingled and I felt myself tremble with momentary fright. The voice spoke again: "Those goddamned NASA bunglers, we're all about to die anyway."

They were behind schedule, it was true. But even given their failings, nothing could quite justify the acid criticism, the savage personal insult, the vitriol that filled the room for ten minutes as the judge described NASA's response to the crisis. And the rest of the world's. I spare you the details.

In the end, the judge told me, his one regret was that he'd wanted to go out big.

Unix rolled her eyes.

I had to bite my tongue.

"Put me back now, goddamnit," the judge said.

"What does he mean?" I asked.

"He goes with Aunt Keiko," Unix said. "Has to do with body temperature."

"We'll rest now," Keiko said. "Thank you, Cooper, for coming by."

I held out my hand forlornly, and Keiko touched it briefly before turning to be alone with her husband. The look in her eyes confirmed that I had lost her, absolutely, to a 117-year-old man the size of a tomato seed. And a mean-spirited bastard besides. Perhaps that's what it took to cling so tenaciously to life.

Keiko opened the top of her hospital gown and slipped him down into her bosom. Out of respect I tried not to stare.

Unix looked at me with raised eyebrows. "For him, it's the adventure of a lifetime." Then she swallowed and looked alarmed at having let slip an off-color remark.

Embarrassed for her, I blurted out, "Finally conclusive proof that size isn't everything." It was really a stupid joke, but Unix looked at me gratefully while Keiko pretended not to hear, turned with dignity to leave the room.

Unix put her hand on my back. "Say, Coop," she said.

It must have been the comet.

Unix walked me out to my Lotus with a shy batting of her green-lined eyes and thanked me for the way I'd helped her aunt.

"If you only actually knew," I said.

"I know. Look, what counts is, you did the right thing in the end. My aunt's happy; little Caesar is back on his throne. Frankly, I think she's missing a bet. I've thought so from the beginning. Especially now, with your comet in the sky."

Then Unix kissed me, really kissed me.

I kissed back.

She slipped her tongue between my teeth and wiggled it around.

We fell against the car, shamelessly groping at one another, sliding down the hood and along the fender and over the headlight, pulling at one another's clothes, half naked by the time we rolled onto the soft lawn.

What can I say of that first encounter that could do justice to our passion, to the bliss that mixed with relief down through my bones? No words can quite describe the sensation—but oh, the touch of her flesh, the warmth of her breath, that moment of slippery joy.

◇

We went everywhere together for twelve hours, having sex. Like a lot of people. We wound up in the boardroom on the eightieth floor of the GD Tower. I felt wonderful, lying there on the slate table, my black Italian wingtips unlaced on the floor, a cashmere sweater rolled into a pillow beneath my head, Unix's thigh inches from my teeth.

On the wallscreen new infomercials for our *Purgatorio* offering produced by Fiat/Disney were running. I hadn't quite understood the attraction of appearing periodically throughout eternity suffering one of the punishments of Purgatory, but when I saw the actress Candy Candiotti jogging around the Fourth *Cornice* to show her victory over Sloth, I realized that *Purgatorio* would sell out completely, too.

Later that morning I showed Unix around corporate headquarters; for all the volume Max said we were doing, you'd have thought GD Inc. was shutting down. The business floors were almost deserted, the Angel® Imaging Center on skeleton crew, all but one of Resurrection Chapel's Dial-a-Faith windows dark. The usual staff was working in Preparation, but the Motor Pool was quiet, and there were only two girls down in Floral. I'd called off my franchisee classes. I took Unix through the Professional Education wing, looked into the great room. When I saw the clock on the wall at eleven, I felt a pang of guilt, felt I ought to be working.

It passed. *Let the dead attend to themselves a bit*, I remember thinking. Unix and I went up two floors and wandered into the Casket Selection Suite. We wound up unraveling a dozen bolts of satin and tunneling into a love nest of pillows. The funeral business, more so than other work, gives you an enhanced appreciation for life.

In the late afternoon we were back up on the slate table again. The Obit Channel was still running on the far wall-screen.

"Coop," Unix said. "What's that?"

A news flash was crawling across the bottom of the screen, text shot through with a red comet icon:

> ... authorities are investigating reports that changes to comet Virgilius Maro's trajectory may be linked to a bizarre "lights out" phenomenon in Puerto Rico on Sunday. Near Arecibo, an unknown hacker diverted the entire electrical supply of the island to the site of the SETI transmitter for more than thirty minutes ...

◇

"Lance'll fix it," Max said. "He's very sorry, but he and that friend of his down there..."

"*Lance*. What happened?"

"It's called a steering pulse, Uncle Coop, a microwave thing? Beam it up there. We heat up one side of the comet, see, fiddle with its spin. We needed to move the orbit just a tad closer to earth to get the resolution we needed? The one we contracted for with Fiat/Disney?"

"So they miscalculated a bit," Max said. "They're just students. They'll fix it, don't get too upset. Hell, it's unbelievably great for us. You see the Obit Channel numbers? We're kickin' butt."

By then society had ceased normal functioning; people stayed home from their jobs, construction projects went on hold, kids skipped school. But the cities were surprisingly peaceful. (Of course, it was still early in that historic week.) Those were the days when traffic thinned and industries all but shut down around the world and the air cleared. We all awaited the delayed launch from the Cape. A back-up was in position as well. We tried not to worry.

◇

The business, you will appreciate, was entirely out of my hands. Cash and electronic transfer money flowed into GD Inc.'s accounts like water from a dozen fire hoses. On Wednesday I logged into the firm's proprietary accounting program to see what Max had been up to with FEMA. In the face of disaster, he'd been playing the market both ends against the middle. He'd contracted with FEMA to service millions of potential fatalities, but he'd so far underbid the competition that our losses would be greater than our net worth if we had to deliver from even a glancing blow of the comet. Meanwhile, the virtual studios were holotaping IMMORTALITY NOW! segments on double shifts throughout the country.

The actual work continued to stall. The dead continued to go unburied in coolers. The great room, the walks with my students, the lectures on setting features, the insertions of the Mona Lisa® smiles, these were out of my life now. Some heroic funerals were being conducted: we did our part, sending our maglev Fleetwoods out undermanned, deploying mobile embalming centers, express shipping corpses around the country on chartered flights if it was too difficult for surviving family to travel.

You don't need me to tell you that the story of those times was an epic adventure which all of us helped write. I'll confine myself to finishing the inside story of the comet, since that was what changed your life, too.

As you've probably surmised, Lance was counting on a fix of the comet's path but not getting results. And, as you remember from that week, on the morning of the great launch, the unmanned shuttle carrying the Ukrainian warheads to the "factory in space" blew up all but a dozen of the backup nukes on the pad. Then there was the problem with the guidance system on the backup shuttle, which knocked the "factory-in-space" out of orbit and eventually back down to earth. Thankfully no one was hurt. The Chinese still say that problem with the guidance system was caused by broadband radio noise pulsing somewhere out of the Caribbean. Lance denies it.

I remember hearing about the collision between the backup

shuttle and the Chinese "factory-in-space" at Espagio's—one of the few restaurants left open—where I'd gone for lunch with Unix. I took a call from Max immediately afterwards.

Max said, "Do you want the good news or bad news first?"

"The bad news I just heard for myself. According to NASA we've got just one more chance, with just one more nuke and that old launch vehicle from Vandenberg. They're cutting it close—going straight for the comet. I'm worried."

"Then let me cheer you up. *Inferno* sales are through the roof. We've got clients wallowing around in frozen garbage in the circle of the gluttons, women biting one another, employees getting their bosses sunk in shit. What a good idea."

I'd seen for myself, watched a famous criminal, the Organ Bandit, writhing happily in flames in the Circle of Thieves. The punishment was only staged, but his eternal celebrity promised to be real.

"One more thing," Max said. "We've made our greatest placement ever. Lance found out they had room for half a kilo more payload on that last emergency attempt to blow the comet off course. So we bought the spot in the nose cone."

"And what in the name of God are we going to do with that?"

"We'll be sending up a cremate. It's like burial at sea, but much grander."

"Who could have the vanity...?"

"That judge," Max told me, "what's his name? MacPhee."

I recall it was Thursday night of that week when society started becoming really unglued—lawlessness swept the beaches, looting raged on Rodeo Drive, anarchy on the freeways. Public safety followed public transport into frightened hibernation. But the weather turned gorgeous—the air crystal clear and the stars shining brightly that night when the whole power grid went down, the stars of the Milky Way lighting the bowl of the sky with celestial jewelry.

I braved the streets to Westwood on Friday.

Keiko was fortified at the mansion, spending her last days with the judge. Max had arranged for a cortege of armored hearses to transport the judge up the coast to Vandenberg Air Force Base for the launch when the time came.

When I looped back through downtown I found Max and Lance camped out up in accounting. Business was still streaming in; Max had Lance shunting in overload invoice servers into the corporate mainframe. Max was filled with enthusiasm for the judge's journey as payload on the third rocket, but guarded about the details, as if he didn't trust me with them. A marketing vision of cosmic proportions danced in his eyes: GD's greatest triumph, he told me, the beginning of a whole new range of franchise-level services, symbolic of his joining with Lance.

Then fires began to smoke the atmosphere. From the eightieth floor window I watched a sooty cloud rise from South Central, then a fireline start further south, by Long Beach Harbor, where Nomads lived on boats. The winds were pulling the smoke across the whole basin. Even as I watched, a string of brush fires ignited above Malibu.

That's when we flew to Mauna Kea, Unix and I.

Since the late twentieth century, Mauna Kea, crowned by the Thirty Meter Telescope, has been the premier optical and infrared imaging site on the globe. Fourteen thousand feet high, isolated by thousands and thousands of miles of Pacific Ocean from the nearest landmass, Mauna Kea is impacted only by air pollution downstream from China, a high mustard haze which that week had slowly dissolved into nothingness.

It is a rugged site, rust-red and black with lava ash and boulders, the fixed observatories on their little knolls, a gravel road winding up from the astronomer's quarters a few thousand feet below. I found out I could image from the summit itself, a cinder cone a kilometer east of the large TMT instrument. Unix and I staked out a spot and I deployed my small imaging package on the night we arrived. By midnight I'd set celestial coordinates, and we settled in.

We had a little self-erecting tent and good down bags, picnic hampers of food, our own satlink to watch the madness back on the mainland. But mostly we watched the sky, rich with stars, the great silver swipe of *Virgilius Maro* wide across the heavens, Mars and Venus bumping one another on the horizon, as if jostling to get out of the way. The firmament seemed a vast deep blue bowl; up there, with the sky so clear and nothing around you, you feel yourself suspended in space, a cosmic traveler.

We thought we could make out the launch of the Vandenberg rocket, its passage through the ionosphere. "Uncle's up there," I heard Unix whisper in wonder.

Unix and I grew very close. Our zipped-together bags made a womb from which we emerged only late on the final day.

As you know, the nuke merely turned *Virgilius Maro* off course. It wasn't the way it might have been in an old SF movie, blowing up. No, that would have sent fragments in the direction of Earth. Rather, it was a flash, albeit a diamond bright human flash, and then the turning, the quickening across the sky.

I don't mean to diminish it. What a night that was: the thrill of the comet turning, the colors spreading across the heavens, refracted light in bands of red and orange and water blue, Unix against my side, my equipment whirring... It was lovelier, and more dangerous, than any other moment I have experienced.

The comet streaked across the sky, some cosmic fulfillment, an instrument, a sign of change for myself, for the world I lived in. As the rocket had slivered into the comet's albedo, as the nuke had blossomed, as the shifting colors had climaxed, I'd tracked the nearby click of servos and the squeaks of optical drives to confirm my hopes: my equipment had grabbed just the right fourteen seconds.

In the ensuing silence we stood there, Unix and I, our breaths vaporizing before us, the cold rock hard beneath our feet, our hearts beating together. I cannot tell you how happy I felt at that moment, how fulfilled.

My pager hummed against my heart.

I took the call through the backup monitor on my imaging equipment, my chilly fingers fumbling with the thin lead. Keesha was on the tiny screen. She looked stricken.

She was calling to tell me that Max Sczyczypek was dead, of massive cardiac arrest.

◇

You of course know all about the unexpected effects of the near miss—that tidal thing, the way the ozone layer was restored to pre-1900 levels, the way the lower atmosphere cleared. I remember the day after we returned to California, waking up and gazing through the clear, crisp air that had been with us since the comet passed. The rapid ionization of the atmosphere had picked up the particulates and plopped them on the ground, where they were washed by heavy rains; the world seemed fresh and new. It changed all our lives, that near-death experience.

Max, as I've mentioned, got a little nearer than most.

His funeral was one of the most spectacular and professionally accomplished in the modern history of deathcare management. It was understood that I would handle the basic interment, though I left the stainless steel instruments, the needles, the gloves and the fluids to Preparation. I dressed Max in his best black suit, picked out a casket, and laid him out, setting his features with a number six Mona Lisa® smile. Dorothy helped me with his obituary; the Sierra Club managed the flowers and the stands of virgin Redwood offered in his name, Espagio's did the catering, Fiat/Disney produced the wake and the procession. The High Mass was held at St. Christopher's, with a little virtual hookup to all GD Homes. Burial was at St. Mary's: Digger O'Donald was there, an orchestra, celebrities by the hundreds, with a special presentation by the union of professional mourners Max himself had helped found.

That was when I first spotted the chemistry between Unix and Lance. I was surprised but then it seemed to me a good thing. I wasn't sure I could keep up with her, and she needed someone who looked further ahead than I do these days.

Lance and I run the company now. Max left us very well off. We have all that front money from FEMA in the bank, all those fees from IMMORTALITY NOW! without the liability to produce it as advertised. Since the comet had been redirected by the Government under an action classified by the courts as an Act of God or War, our warrantee must exclude any mention of "comet." No comet, no signal. The broadband noise that had been converted into holounits from *The Divine Comedy* would continue to be broadcast by the redirected *Virgilius Maro*, but only in the path of the M31 Galaxy for the next four hundred million years.

We *own* the Obit Channel now—under a dummy corporation, however those things are done. All of the Angels® have been dusted, the Fleetwoods shine, and our new South American division is expanding at the rate of two new Homes per week.

I still feel deep satisfaction with the image I'd grabbed of *Virgilius Maro* up on Mauna Kea. During the final edit I doubled the length of the hololoop. The finished piece hangs in the boardroom these days, replacing an image of Mars. The now half-minute loop, bright silver with a banded spectrum in slo-mo, opens and turns like a timelapse flower bathing in quasar light against a backdrop of deep space.

I see Keiko a lot. It's a bit unreal. Lance and Unix are a couple. We're all into life extension. Lance is working with those Swiss engineers you've been hearing about on the news. I mean, why not stick with a good thing?

One more thing I'll need to tell you about.

After all the dust had settled, Keiko and Unix and Lance and I took what remained of the judge's ashes and placed them into a crypt. He had refused to take his ashes up with him to Vandenberg; he'd called it a morbid idea. The left-behind ashes had been moved to GD Tower, but Keiko understandably wanted closure. Burial was my advice, a small traditional service; I was glad to see my thinking confirmed by Keiko's therapist and the MacPhee family counselor. The obsequies were set for a Friday afternoon.

I set out driving alone in my Lotus from downtown to meet the rest of the funeral party at Forest Lawn. I'd picked up the ashes from GD Tower and was carrying them on the passenger's seat. They were resting in a beautiful onyx urn. I rounded a corner, my suspension let out a squeak, a groan, and I found myself remembering my first encounter with the judge's ashes in the Model 986 Urn. I started seeing him as a rival again. Instinctively, I reached for the glove box, pulled out the plastic bag containing the ashes of Balthazar, my old Lab, and exchanged them for the ashes of the judge. The idea that the urn containing the judge's ashes would make a noise during interment spooked me more than I can explain. I know what I did was unethical; I couldn't help myself.

Anyway, the modest ceremony went well. Unix had arranged for Scottish Pipers, and a representative from NASA stood in uniform and saluted. Keiko achieved her closure.

The thing is, after the dinner at Espagio's, when I was driving back to Westwood with Keiko, swinging up Santa Monica Boulevard?

I swear I heard something from the glovebox: a creak, a pop, a long high note that sang eerily into the gathering night.

Keiko looked at me.

"Balthazar," I said. "Hush."

GEROPODS

Grow old along with me, the best of life is yet to be…
– *Browning*

Like me, my two elderly companions had outlived their wives, but I was new to Arcadia. You know the sort of place I'm talking about, somewhere between a nursing home and a morgue: pastel walls with prints of rolling hills in "quality" antiqued frames, sturdy plastic furniture, a tiled, low-maintenance floor. That afternoon, the digital holo in the corner of the sunroom was tuned to THE YOUNG AND THE OLD, a trendy soap starring the ancient McCauley Culkin, his already pale colors so washed out by the late afternoon glare he looked transparent. The air was laced with the odors of antiseptic and urine. Distant rattling and the indistinct conversations of the old echoed through the complex chip-array hearing aid I wore like a baseball cap.

I'd come out of a long stay in the hospital—my total deafness aside, a Parkinson's-like movement disorder was getting the best of me. Pinkie and I hadn't had any kids. After a long career as a shrink, it looked like I'd moved into my final home.

"*Bored*?" Kaplan said from his wheelchair. "Are you kidding? I used to be a Hollywood agent. Bored? It's so boring here it must be a new medical condition, right?"

"That evidence is accepted by this court," Judge Ortiz said from the couch, waving his red and white striped cane. The dot from its laser guidance flew around the room like a bug.

"I had depressives who literally put me to sleep," I recalled from my practice. "But, OK, maybe we do break new ground here. The question is, what's the alternative? We're disabled and technically incompetent. The law says we can't leave."

"Not quite right," Kaplan said. "Judge, tell him about Geropods."

"Geropods?"

The Judge shushed me in a conspiratorial way as an orderly cruised in behind a trolley rattling with glass and plastic. I already knew him as Dennis, his hair the color of straw, his neck wider than his ears. He passed me my dopamine agonists in a little plastic cup and ticked his stylus on his palm chart. "DIDN'T SEE YOU AT THE LUAU LAST NIGHT, DOC," Dennis shouted, as if my hat was out of order.

"That's because I *lived* in Hawaii during the Aussie war," I muttered, watching my hand shake and water splash out of the cup. "Luau Night here is pathetic. Hawaii without the beach."

"*Exactly*," Judge Ortiz agreed.

Kaplan swung his wheelchair around, just missing Dennis' shin. "Casino Night without the money," he chimed in. "Casting without the couch."

Dennis, who'd gone a bit pink, tucked the palm chart into the trolley. "Valentine's Day coming up," he said ingenuously. "Let's see. That would be sex without the…"

Kaplan pumped his arms and nailed him across both shins with quick reverse sweep of his chair.

"Re … strictions …," Dennis hissed when he could speak. "Going to talk to … Nurse Tucker… Re … strict … you all from … recreation … room…"

When we were alone again, Kaplan rolled over to the Judge. "All right, *tell* him about Geropods. The Doc's been in the hospital."

"OK," said Judge Ortiz. "Supreme Court decision last month. Civil rights case brought by the AARP. You're correct; the law says we can't leave as individuals—danger to ourselves, incompetent, all that crap. *But* the Court also ruled that any *group* of infirm old people whose *combined* physical and mental capacities constitute the powers of a single, competent individual, is collectively entitled to act *as* an individual, as a single, legally defined human being."

"A Geropod," Kaplan chimed in. "Free as a blue jay."

"Justice Kirkpatrick's term," Ortiz said. "I'm blind, but Kaplan here can see. Kaplan's in a wheelchair, but you're ambulatory. As a matter of fact, you're the one who's going to move us around."

"Me?"

"We've been looking for a guy like you. Of course, you're stone deaf without your hat, and you goddamned vibrate all the time…"

"Parkinson's…"

"So you need help yourself. But among us we've got all the parts."

"And where would we go?"

"Mr. Kaplan has a *burning mission,*" the Judge told me, his face swinging from side to side.

"My daughter Monica," Kaplan explained, "is in her late forties. Five years ago she marries a client of mine, 'Boots' Bacci. From that talk show on the moon? Remember him? Always wore silver boots? I get admitted into Cedars with a stroke, the snake talks me into signing over the house in Brentwood. I get released from Cedars, and instead of taking me home, he gets behind my wheelchair, crams me into his sports car, then pushes me in here."

"Time for a little payback," Judge Ortiz said, pushing on his cane and rising from the couch. "Are you with us?"

A sharp animal sound, a yapping, came from the direction of the lobby. I adjusted my cap, feeling a bit frail. My companions didn't strike me as completely stable, but… "Is that a dog?"

"No, it's a Yorkshire terrier. Animal therapy day."

I like animals, but I recalled how the previous week a pot-bellied pig had fouled the library floor. "I'm with you, gents. Let's roll."

◇

And so I stood there the next morning, shaking on my walker, leaning on the gurney, fresh air just ten feet away. Dennis was scanning our forms into the web station with a frown, Nurse Tucker looking over his shoulder. Partly because we were dressed in street clothes, my two partners in old suits, myself in cords and a cardigan, we'd attracted a bit of a crowd. There was Agnes Dorchester with her humped back and blue nightgown, Ted Makelena with his robe pockets filled with sweets, Marjorie Walters in her ridiculous tracksuit.

Nurse Tucker grimaced over the terminal. "What about him?" she asked, pointing to the gurney that Kaplan had instructed me to push.

"He's with us. Tiger Montelban," Judge Ortiz said. Even I remembered him as a screen playboy. He'd been Kaplan's most productive client.

"Medical data's in order, but what's he do for your 'pod? He's been comatose for a year."

"He can pee, which I can't," Kaplan said. "Wanna see my catheter?"

Tucker rolled her eyes. Actually, so did I.

"Look here," the Judge snapped. "It doesn't matter if he can do anything. The law says that the sum of our powers merely has to replicate those of a normal adult."

Tucker sighed, puzzled over the terminal, then it beeped. "Admin says you guys can go," she said with quiet surprise. "What name?" As a new single legal entity, we had to provide a separate name.

"Story Musgrave," the Judge answered. Musgrave had been my idea. The bald ex-marine, one of the first astronauts, had been active into his nineties, had six graduate degrees including one in medicine, and at ninety-seven was with the crew that went to Mars.

The sliding doors opened, and we took our first step through.

◇

It was surprisingly easy going at first. We weren't fast, exactly, but the gurney I was pushing stabilized my tremor and provided a platform for Judge Ortiz to walk along as he tapped his way. Kaplan was out in front, leading us to the parking lot. He'd been savvy enough to hire a van, a big one, into whose capacious back the driver helped us slide Tiger Montelban's gurney.

I took a deep breath and smelled the hot pavement, the wet grass under the sprinklers. I heard noise from traffic on Wilshire, and, yes, birds!, so loud I had to turn down my hat. The sunlight was amazing, the sky huge. I knew Pinkie would have been proud of me. I swung closed the rear door. "Why *are* we taking this guy along?" I wondered.

"Kaplan said he owed him one last ride," Ortiz shrugged. "Now help me in."

At the Judge's suggestion, Miguel, our driver, first drove us toward the Pacific at Venice, then through the park in Santa Monica and up along the beach in Malibu. Ortiz had his head out the window like a Lab, his thin hair streaming in the wind. What a pleasure it was to ride along the blue ocean, the wide stretches of sand, to see the girls on their maglev boards weaving down pedestrian tracks. Trees! Dogs! People whose hair wasn't white! At a crosswalk, an infant in a stroller made me realize how much I'd missed seeing children. When we turned back toward the city, I rolled down my own window and caught a scent on the breeze and remembered something else: Mexican food!

But before we could eat, Kaplan insisted, we had an assignment at his house in Brentwood.

"What's the plan?" I asked, not for the first time. The night before, Kaplan had prattled about "degrading assets," but he hadn't been entirely clear. I had him diagnosed as manic, the judge as suffering from cerebral arteriosclerosis, one of whose side effects is senile dementia. I suppose I had a touch of that myself.

"First step, we shake him up. Ground zero, the garage," Kaplan said. "That sports car of his? He's got one of the first fuel-cell Lamborghinis. The model that looks like a shuttle?"

I sucked in air between my teeth. "We'd stoop to petty vandalism?"

"No no no no. He loves that car more than he loves Monica. It's his financial security, see? His first two wives got all his money, and it's the only asset he has. Aside from my daughter." From a pocket of his wheelchair, Kaplan extracted a small black case. "I've still got a remote for the garage," he whispered.

"And?"

From another pocket, he pulled a spray can with an ugly, mustard-colored top. "Think you can handle this, Doc?" he said with glee. "The idea is, I open the door, then we... well, you ... decorate the Lamborghini."

I raised a shaking hand. So vandalism it was. My first impulse was to refuse, but then I took a deep breath ... and imagined Pinkie laughing. So what if we got caught? And maybe we could get it over with, quick, like a prostate exam. We could have a wonderful day. "And then?" I asked.

Kaplan hesitated, his eyes glazed with confusion.

"And then the rest of the plan develops," Ortiz said gamely. He was still half out his open window, the breeze on his face, a self-absorbed smile on his lips. "We take it one step at a time."

◇

From a block away, Kaplan's house looked to be an impressive small mansion in the Tudor style. It had a gabled portico, two stories with a large east wing, a sizeable pool and a cabana in the side yard, and a four-car garage.

"Somebody's there!" Kaplan choked. Miguel pulled along the curb, and I watched a heavyset man heave himself out of the pool. I saw him slip on silver sandals and with a shock recognized that it was Boots Bacci himself. He had put on a lot of weight since he'd returned to Earth's gravity, and the way he scratched his ample belly, he was not expected at the studio anytime soon. He pushed his wet black hair back, and it seemed to lift from his scalp.

"Say, how old's that guy?" I asked.

"Sixty-eight," Kaplan muttered. "You'd think he'd have more consideration, right?"

Boots bent toward his towel and sunglasses, picked up a script, threw the towel around his shoulders, looked toward the street. He cast a quick, hostile glance at our van, and walked into the house.

We could follow his progress through a side window, see him step half naked into a small room, ease his dripping body into a leather chair, hoist his feet up...

"My teak desk," Kaplan said in a small, unhappy voice.

Then Boots pointed a remote toward the window and closed the blinds.

Kaplan had Miguel move up the block, putting a stand of bright pink oleander between us and his house.

Kaplan and Ortiz started bickering. Under the pretext of a battery problem, I took off my hat and fiddled with it as they talked. That's the one thing, the only thing, about my deafness for which I am grateful: I don't have to hear anything I don't want to hear. You can imagine what that did to my psychiatric practice toward the end. Now, though I'd lost confidence in Kaplan, I was still glad to be away from Arcadia. My jiggling foot tapped a rhythm on the van's floorboards.

After a while I realized that Kaplan was shouting at me.

"I can hear you now," I said, adjusting my hat.

Kaplan ordered Ortiz and me out, got out himself, and dispatched Miguel back to the house. His mission was to ring the doorbell and ascertain if Monica was at home. Kaplan's idea was that if she was home, we could discreetly enter through a side door and occupy the screening room, where we could lock ourselves in. The plan sounded lame.

Turned out *she* was at work, at her desk at the William Morris Agency in Studio City. And Boots Bacci made it clear to Miguel that if "that van" didn't "evaporate" from the neighborhood, he was calling the cops.

"Do you think he made us?" the Judge asked as Miguel put the van in gear.

“I tol’ him we was gardeners. You know, mow and blow?”

“Where now?” the Judge asked.

“Weapons,” Kaplan said. “Tasers. Pipe bomb.”

“Dios,” Miguel muttered under his breath.

“You’re obsessing, Marv,” I told Kaplan in my best professional voice. “You’re going to give yourself another stroke. I prescribe lunch.”

“All right, Miguel,” Kaplan said with dismay. “Head for Casa Escobar. On Alvarado Street.”

The new “old” Mexican part of town, for all its advertised ethnic uniqueness, looked a lot like the Beverly Hills Mall. Half the buildings were sand-colored stucco, with heavy black timbers, Mission-style arches, and red tiled roofs. Many of the arches opened onto recessed mini-malls disguised as blocks of market stalls. Miguel maneuvered us into a disabled parking space, and we formed our pod again, Ortiz and Montelban and I in a wedge behind Kaplan’s wheelchair.

We moved through the crowd fronting Pescado Mojado like a tanker in heavy seas, past Selena World, past Hologames R Us, past Alberto’s Secret. I had forgotten the theme park domesticity of the new old part of town, the fountains, the fishponds, the forests of cacti and rented ficus, the tidy upscale families with their matching body studs. Interiors were uniformly dense with epiphytes and those sheet-water walls that have become so big. Really, I hate it when I accidentally lean against one.

“Whoa,” I head Kaplan shout. “Senoritas at eleven o’clock!”

I looked ahead. Three elderly women were pushing along a narrow white table high with what I took to be catered food.

“What’s he talking about?” Ortiz asked.

“*Senoritas,*” Kaplan said. “Babes.”

“Good grief,” I said. “They’re pushing a gurney.”

"Tell me what they look like," Ortiz said.

"They look as old as we are. Except the one in front—Kaplan's right—she's some ... babe. Big blue hair, leopard-skin outfit, wide black belt, gold high heels. Great legs. Behind her, alongside the gurney, there's a woman who looks like ... I guess you'd say a giant robin. Big bosom, big behind. Grandmotherly. She's got a red and white striped cane. Laser guidance."

"Come to Papito," I heard Ortiz say to my surprise.

"The thin one on the other side reminds me of Pinkie. My late wife. She's using one of those electric canes. That woman up front, though. She's got to be somebody's daughter."

"Faster, Doc," Kaplan urged, leaning forward into his wheelchair and pushing hard. "Let's cut them off at Orange Julio's."

"An all-woman Geropod?" Judge Ortiz marveled. "I'm absolutely charmed."

"Such a gentleman," the blind woman replied, feeling around the table discreetly for her Venison Burrito with one hand, fingering the straw in her fluorescent green Margarita with the other.

We were clustered at the rear of Casa Escobar. There'd been some trouble about the gurneys, but we arranged to park them just outside, in a quiet alcove with a little birdbath. To my great relief, the woman who reminded me of Pinkie turned out to be a retired intensive care nurse. Between us we checked vital signs on Tiger and started a new IV line on her temporary patient, a one-hundred-and-twenty-year-old woman whose hair was so white, whose still smile was so beatific, she looked like a porcelain angel.

Kaplan had settled deep into the red booth alongside the woman with the blue hair. Her name was Bette. Her makeup was very thick, but expertly applied. She was as old as the rest of us, it turned out, and a marvel. Her artificial lungs gave her a breathy voice and she'd somehow managed to keep her figure, or at least had tucked and squeezed it into the leopard skin suit in a way that belied her age. Unless you looked closely, you might have easily mistaken her for a woman in her early fifties.

"Were you in the industry?" Kaplan asked. "Films? Holos?"

"I was on a poster once," she said coyly.

"If you'd had the right representation..." Kaplan speculated, flattering her in the easy way of an experienced professional.

Bette's false eyelashes fluttered so vigorously I thought I felt a breeze.

And so we ate and talked. By the time it came to coffee and flan, the restaurant was almost empty. Ostensibly to try one another's laser canes, Ortiz and the blind woman groped their way into a separate booth for dessert.

The ex-nurse and I went out to the alcove to check on our charges again. Her name was Barbara.

"So how do you like being old?" I asked, adjusting my hat.

"Today is fun," she said. "But it's hard to do things."

I nodded. "I suppose I had some training. In med school they had us put on scratched-up goggles—like we had cataracts. Plugged our ears with wax, gave us heavy rubber gloves..."

"Like arthritis."

"Put marshmallows in our mouths..."

"Mmmm. Post stroke paralysis."

"... corn kernels in our shoes, braces around our necks. The worst thing was the padded diapers."

She laughed and blushed. "Let me guess. They had you try to read prescription labels with the goggles on, count out pills with fat fingers, eat around the marshmallows."

"Exactly."

"In nursing school, we had to spend a morning in a hospital bed, got applesauce shoved into our mouths every half hour. Isn't it great to be out here?"

"Want to walk down Alvarado?" I asked.

It took us forever, but not since Pinkie died have I spent such a pleasant hour with a woman. We lingered in Casa DIY, admiring the lawn furniture and the barbecue grills. Outside Burrito Loco her electric cane got confused by a passing mag lev scooter. She started to stumble, and I reached out to hold her arm to steady her.

When she regained her balance, she slipped her warm fingers into mine, and we made our way back down the sidewalk holding hands.

"I'd give you my heart," she said as we approached the restaurant, "but it's plastic and I think it needs a new battery."

I laughed. "Like my kidney," I said. "But how about if I ask you for a date sometime?"

◇

Back at the big red booth in Casa Escobar, Kaplan announced that he had a plan.

"I hope you don't have too much for me to do," I admitted. "I'm bushed."

"Not necessary," Kaplan said. "Bette here's going in."

Kaplan explained that he'd sent Miguel over to the office supply store next door and was faxing over some forged NASA stationery from an FX vault he used to work with. The idea was to mock up a letter from Story Musgrave Junior to Boots Bacci—as Kaplan recalled, Junior had been a guest on Boots' talk show some years earlier during a tribute to his dad. The letter would personally introduce Bette as a talented performer whose career just wanted the kind of help Bacci could provide through his extensive contacts. "Let's see," Kaplan muttered as he scribbled notes. "We'll put in something about using Boots to host an old astronaut special. 'Please give this warm lady your special attention, the Boots Bacci boost we all know about, that big, stiff rocket…'"

Bette was going to take a cab and present herself at the front door of the Brentwood house with the letter in hand.

Kaplan set down his notes. "Then we let Nature take its course."

"What was—uh, is—your career?" I asked Bette.

"She was an exotic dancer," Barbara giggled.

"Use what you've got, honey," Bette said. "Just get me to Casa Charo on the way so's I can get a blonde wig and some sunglasses. And I'd like another Margarita."

Kaplan was radiant. "She's gonna be a star."

We all wanted to be there in Brentwood, if only down the block, to see if she'd get into the house. But were stumped about the gurneys.

"We could get arrested for harassment," the Judge said. "I'd hate to see them in a cell."

Barbara pointed out that our charges had been in comas for months. Kaplan said he didn't see anything wrong with leaving the gurneys side by side in the alcove, and giving the busboy a hundred dollars to page us if there was any noticeable change in their condition.

The busboy was not only willing, but even trained in CPR. Though it was a little irresponsible, Barbara and I went along. Kaplan hacked away at the letter, and when it was finished, Miguel moved the van around and helped us in.

I really was tired. There in the back of the van, I settled in for a bit of a nap. I woke up with the mid-afternoon sun in my eyes and realized that we'd stopped. My companions were hushed. When I looked down the street, I saw a blonde in a leopard skin outfit at the front door of the Brentwood house—the blonde was Bette—falling into a big hug from Boots Bacci and being ushered in.

"I still don't get it," I admitted.

From the front of the van, Kaplan placed a call to Studio City, telling Monica that Boots had had a seizure and was unable to get out of bed and that she needed to rush right home.

What really frosted Monica, she told us later, was the way Boots hadn't even folded back the family quilt (an heirloom in colorful interlocking circles, the classic "wedding ring" pattern). When she burst in, distraught, limping on a shoe whose high heel she'd broken during her breathless climb up the stairs, he was sitting right on it, back against the teak headboard, stark naked except for the silk bathrobe Monica had only recently given him for Christmas (strike two). From behind a handheld holocorder, he was apparently directing Bette in some sort of "audition" (strike three). The holodisc, of course, left as little doubt about his guilt as the famous bin Laden tape from before the Aussie War. In a somewhat empty tribute to virtue, leggy Bette had never in fact had to get out of her leopard-skin outfit, which was probably just as well, even though she'd closed the drapes and dimmed the lights. Monica confessed that the affair confirmed growing suspicions she'd had about her husband, who had been taking uncommon interest in a series of female trainers though he never seemed to exercise, and had started locking himself in the screening room.

From the street, the sequence was elegant in its economy —Monica running in the front door, Boots ejected from the rear, hopping past the pool and cabana, struggling to pull on his clothes. He nearly lost it all together when Kaplan punched the garage door's remote.

There were repercussions, of course. Bacci maintained that he had been harassed, entrapped, and defrauded. Before the day was out, we actually had to answer some questions posed to us by an investigator at the LA prosecutor's office.

Bacci himself was there, his eyes puffy, his silver boots scuffed, his anger palpable. He'd inflicted a long scrape on the side of the silver Lamborghini as he'd peeled out of the garage.

"OK," the investigator, an anorexic attorney, began, "Who's Story Musgrave?"

"I am," the Judge said.

"I am," Kaplan added, then he pointed to me.

I waved. "Did you say Story Musgrave?" I asked, adjusting my cap. "That's me."

She sighed. "Mr. Bacci maintains that earlier today, February 7th, you gentlemen, particularly Mr. Kaplan and Judge Ortiz, colluded to defraud him. Now, Mr. Kaplan, I want you to tell me your precise whereabouts from the hours of…"

"Excuse me," he interrupted. "Let's cut to the chase. The medical record will show that I have suffered a massive, debilitating stroke, and the legal record will show that specialists under Mr. Bacci's own supervision had me declared incompetent as an individual not six months ago. Any testimony I might give can't have standing in the State of California."

"Mmm," she mused, consulting her softscreen for a long moment. Then she turned to me. "Doctor, did you hear any conversation between Mr. Kaplan and Judge Ortiz that would suggest such a conspiracy?"

I fiddled with my cap. "Would you please put your question in writing?" I asked.

When she did so, I read the sentence, fiddled with my hat again, and replied. "I'm so sorry for the trouble, counselor. I was trained to be a good listener, but, you see, I've become stone deaf, and my hat's not entirely reliable. So I could hardly…"

"Judge Ortiz," she said, looking down at her softscreen again, sucking her upper lip. "Did you see anything today to call into question the legal standing of the woman known as Bette Waters as a legitimate entertainer seeking professional advice from Mr. Bacci?"

Ortiz twirled his red and white cane, and a bright red dot flew around the room. The dot finally got her attention. "Justice is blind," he said, setting his cane on the floor and rising. "Now can we go?"

That hour at the prosecutor's office, however, wasn't the strangest thing that happened toward the end of that day. Miguel, who said he'd never had a better time in his life, and who still is with us as our driver, ran us back to Casa Escobar to retrieve the gurneys.

They were there in the alcove, all right. But Tiger Montelban wasn't, and neither was the 120-year-old lady.

The busboy was distraught. He'd checked every quarter hour, he told us. He'd been a bit late just after five because he'd had to help set up for dinner. When he'd finally looked in the alcove, they were gone—the tops of the gurneys empty landscapes of rumpled sheets and dented pillows punctuated by a trailing IV line. The restaurant staff had searched the neighborhood. People on the street spoke of an elderly couple in white who looked to be romantically involved, but it was just impossible. There was no report back at the nursing home, nothing from the nearby hospitals, nothing from the police or the morgue. To this day, we don't have a clue to what happened to them, except for a series of charges that appeared on Montelban's credit chip at a resort in Cabo San Lucas. The chip had been embedded in his wrist.

These days we count on Arcadia for our medical care three days out of every seven, but otherwise we spend extended weekends at the house in Brentwood, sitting in leather furniture, watching sports in the den, taking in old movies with Barbara and Bette and Ramona in the screening room—that's really a treat, as Marv has remastered digital holos of all the great ones from the past hundred and fifty years, from *Birth of a Nation* to the twelve Lucas *Star Wars* sequels. Monica's a regular angel, kind and considerate and a world-class caterer, though we do our best to look after ourselves as much as we can.

Barbara and I have taken to light exercise in the pool and lounging beside the cabana. Every once in a while, lying on my back, relaxed and at peace—a third try with stem cells has reduced my tremor—I look up and think of them, Tiger Montelban and his angel. Occasionally I see them in the shapes of clouds rolling in the sky, soft and free as floating gauze or down, white as bright moonlight on a snow-covered mountain, drifting in the heavens together, arm in arm.

ABOUT THE AUTHOR

Robert Onopa was a Fellow of the National Endowment for the Arts. Along with his science fiction, his work appeared in *TriQuarterly, Harper's, the Chicago Tribune, The Singapore Straits-Times, and Zyzzyva.* He has taught at Northwestern, as a Fulbright lecturer in West Africa, and at Victoria University in New Zealand. He is now Professor Emeritus at the University of Hawaii, and lives on the Windward side of Oahu.

www.ingramcontent.com/pod-product-compliance
Lightning Source LLC
LaVergne TN
LVHW090945080826
845145LV00003B/890

* 9 7 8 1 9 4 4 5 2 1 2 3 3 *